OUR JOURNEY TO SUCCESS

OUR JOURNEY TO SUCCESS

Mohamed Al Hamad

and

Ahmed Al Hamad

Copyright

As a tribute to our beloved parents who have spared no effort throughout their lives for us, we dedicate this book and its fulfilments for their unconditional love and support that brought us to our every success. Unfortunately, our late father may not have had the chance to read this book, but we are sure of how proud and happy he is for where we are now and our achievements, as this has been what he wanted us to be his entire life.

We don't follow, we lead.

— Springers, 2018

Contents

Foreword

Looking back twenty years ago when I first knew the two brothers, I did not imagine that they could reach what they have reached today. Knowing their personalities twenty years ago, I cannot say that they were the same people that they are today, but what I can really say and confirm is that once the flame of creativity ignites it will not stop.

Although the age difference between them does not exceed a year, each of them has a different creative personality. Mohamed is the older brother; he is the CEO of the company who is full of vitality and positive energy. He is a glorious, impulsive person to achieve his goals, and he does not follow the traditional or classic style of management. Many may disagree with him with the way he acts or the way he works, but he keeps achieving success after success and is considered an inspiring person to many people. As for Ahmed, he is a torch of activity, a man with an unlimited creativity, and a man with many visions. I can say that he is the right man for the mission impossible.

"There is a brother that your mother did not give birth to." This Arab proverb embodies my situation with the Al Hamad brothers. They are more than brothers to me, as I have known them for more than twenty years. Throughout the years, I was able to stick with them and often close enough to live with them and have been there with all the painful and joyful situations they had, making our closeness and bond increase. For more than half of my life, I was able to know them better and for them to know me clearly as well. The relationship was alternating in terms of my proximity with the two brothers, so I was sometimes closer to Ahmed, whom I knew first, and sometimes I was closer with Mohamed until the level of the relationship stabilized to be the same distance between the two together.

Their success story, which is portrayed in this book in several chapters covering the stages of changes, will show you how their personalities affected their success, when their goals crystallized, when their energy was charged up, and when their determination increased. Despite their rapid rise to the top of the most successful companies in mass tourism, change and success did not affect their loving nature to others, which you will read about in this book. Take inspiration, interest, and lessons from them. Let their story get you sharpened and motivated to achieve your goals, even if you are far away from them. Work hard and love your work no matter what happens.

For those who want to start but are worried about failing, for those who want to move forward but are worried about their past, for those who want to stand but are afraid of falling, all I can say is if you're going to dream, dream big. All big things have a small beginning, and if you fail to prepare, prepare to fail.

Husain Rastam

Business Development Manager

Preface

Time flies so fast. It's like getting onto a flight! We are now approaching the sixth year of Spring Travel. Our first two years were like joining one of our fourteen-day trips—a lot had happened and there are too many memories, as if we had been there for years and years. It felt like we had known everyone for ages.

Spring Travel is not just a successful company, a travel service provider, or a trip to be remembered. It's our own milestone with everyone with us on this journey, and we wanted it to be remembered forever. We built it as our legacy that we want to pass on to the coming generations. It is such a big dream, yet we believe that it is not a dream but a future that we want to build and make our reality.

In the peak of our second summer season's success, we felt that everything just happened so fast that we might miss a memory of it. Our success in the beginning was overwhelming, yet it scared us at the same time, as we gave not only our efforts but our hearts and minds to building and establishing Spring Travel to be one of the leading travel agencies in the Kingdom of Bahrain. We are not dreaming, but we also open our eyes in the fright of reality that a day may come when we bid farewell to this company. This sad reality sparked the idea to write down our history.

Nowadays, technology is so advanced. Everyone relies on the internet, thus making social media play a major role. Ahmed, teaming with our marketing group, decided not to fully get into the cliché of the market by launching collective videos or photos. Instead, he came up with the idea to pen our memories from when we started the business and through the entire history of our journey to success, including publishing our book to be distributed in the entire Kingdom of Bahrain and even to our network worldwide. The book will be something good we can show and pass along to our children, grandchildren, and the following generations. This book will not be just memorabilia to pass on but a chance for us to share in the best how we found success so quickly.

We tell stories of our travels and experiences. We are not writers, and publishing a book is not our area expertise, yet we were swooned into making it possible. The challenges of the idea sparked us to push through, as the uniqueness and pride of being the first travel service company to launch our own book within the country is such a remarkable achievement. Spring

Travel is not just a travel service provider that takes you to places. It is the epitome of inspiration, taking great initiatives and triumphing over challenges. We wanted to showcase Spring Travel as an eye-opener that nothing can limit us from achieving greatness and success.

Acknowledgments

It was not an easy road from the beginning of establishing Spring Travel and Tourism, but we had everyone who supported, lent us their hands, gave out their all-out efforts, and did not spare time that have brought us to our success, making the rise of its name, high in the sky of travel and tourism industry.

Our heartfelt thanks, appreciation, and gratitude to our partner Hasan Sabba. We are immensely grateful for your tremendous trust and support.

Thank you to our hard-working employees, tour captains, and dear family and friends.

Our services wouldn't be top-notch without the strong support of our awesome suppliers such as airlines, hotels, and all tour service providers who massively supported us from the beginning till today.

We are still in awe of the loyal patronage and extreme support that we received and keep receiving from every traveler who entrusted us with his or her holiday, vacation, or business trip.

We are working hard, as always, to provide an excellent service and give every traveler the optimum satisfaction after every trip with us. To our avid travelers, we are deeply grateful for all your support and loyalty. We are striving much more to make sure that we bring you happiness whenever you travel with us.

Writing a book is harder than we thought and more rewarding than we could have ever imagined. None of this would have been possible, and this book would not have materialized without the encouragement, help, guidance, patience, and support of our colleague, Charisse Ann Lim. She stood by us during our struggles and has been part of our success. We're eternally grateful to her.

Finally, we want to express our utmost appreciation and gratitude not just to our best and closest friend but our brother at heart, Husain Rastam, for his undying encouragement, moral support, personal attention, and care.

About the Book

We don't follow. We lead. Spring Travel and Tourism bloomed in the market with the numerous travel agencies. What makes us stand out? We defy the norms and transcend Bahrain's travel market to a whole new level. We are not only leading the travel business in Bahrain, but we also changed and bolstered it up into a diverse trend of traveling.

We don't dream. We live our dreams. Live your dreams, making them reality no matter how many obstacles and struggles block your path. The world has a lot to offer. Travel and discover awaiting surprises. As Springer's vision (Springer is an icon that represents our travel agency), we will take you to great new places you have never been, and together we will explore what the world has to offer us. Our journey to success emboldens and inspires us, as it opens our eyes to a new horizon and gives us the drive to walk toward the road to achieve our goals. Our story will not only ignite you to travel, but it will excite you more with the experience that awaits you by being a part of our groups. Spring is not only a success story to be told but a kind of travel experience.

Chapter 1

Our Beginning

We originally hailed from Manama, rooting from one of the humble families in Al Hamad clan. Our family was an average family with the household consisting of nine siblings and our beloved parents. Our father worked at the Electricity and Water Authority as an electricity meter reader. It was his first job, and he worked it for about ten years till he decided to resign and do taxi transport services with his pickup. Our father spent around twenty years with the taxi service. Sometime in the early 1990s, he decided to stop due to his age, as it was truly tiring for him to continue driving around.

Our father raised us with a hard work ethic, and no age could stop him. Despite his age, our father had to continue working, as he wasn't yet eligible to receive monthly pensions from Social Security. He later became a property broker, finding, selling, and buying land for various property owners. He only received 1 percent commissions for every sold property. The income was not a guaranteed income.

We have massive appreciation for our mother who supported our father by solely taking care of us nine children. She prepared us for school and helped with homework apart from her job as Husaini reciter at ma'atams.

Aside from being a property broker, our father has been engaged in small businesses like a milk shop, cooking gas cylinders, and a cafeteria in Old Manama. Our parents often needed to stretch their earnings for the entire family till the next commissions came. Given the difficult living situation, our father has opened our eyes to many things. As the proverb goes, "Give a man a fish, and you feed him for a day; teach a man to fish, and you feed him for a lifetime." It was not about passing obligations but teaching us how to make a living on our own so we could be good providers in the future for ourselves and our families.

Our teenage years were filled with great memories and life lessons from hardship too. Life is good, but it is never easy. We cannot complain, as we wouldn't be who we are right now without the ups and downs of our lives. It was like a roller-coaster ride. In our younger years, we didn't have the luxury of always having fun or just sitting around, but we were busy building ourselves and our futures.

In 1992, Mohamed was about fourteen years old when our father started making him work in the milk shop in Manama. He was still studying at the time. It became his daily routine till about the end of 1994, roughly two years. He then transferred and worked in our father's cousin's perfume company, and I also started to work in a textile shop. We had the same daily routine for years and years until we began attending university. We would study in the morning, and then we would go directly to the shop and work right after school.

The economic situation in the mid-1990s was not good; the opportunities were extremely limited. Given the situation, it left our father with his hands tied. He strove to provide for our family. Whenever I remember what our dear mother used to tell us about our dear father; it always makes me cry. Our mother told us when we were young that there were times when our father cried at night because he wanted to give us whatever we asked for. It was a hard life for him, struggling and trying to give us what we needed and wanted. I will never forget anything our mother has told us about his sufferings. He couldn't voice his difficulties in front of us. This is why no matter how hard the choices our parents made were, our love and respect for our parents outgrew all the hardships of our younger years. They did their best to give us a good life and to provide us with everything we needed.

It was not easy seeing others the same age as us enjoying their time after school, while we were off to work instead. We could have complained or demanded that they let us do what we wanted. It was tempting, but we could not break our parents' hearts. The hidden emotions in our parents' eyes were enough for us to not be rebellious. The hardships developed a certain character in our personalities to be humble and understanding. We understood why our father had to make us work instead of playing and enjoying our teenage years.

Our parents, especially our father, were in a process of ironing us to be the men he wanted us to be. It was a hard preparation for us. He wanted us to have a better future for ourselves and for our families. Being let out to sea and dealing with different people every day opened our eyes to the reality of life. We understood how life goes—that it won't always come to you as you wanted it to. Instead of complaining about not being able to enjoy our young years, we tried to make use of our time by working and learning from it. It was a groundbreaking experience for me and Ahmed, spending our teenager years working and embracing the hard reality of life. As Ahmed always says, it was one of the most precious teachings our parents have given us, and I couldn't agree more!

Later we realized that it wasn't about working, but it was an opportunity to learn and adapt to life—an opportunity to advance and quench our thirst for bettering ourselves. We are so lucky and will always be proud of our parents. They were an extraordinary couple who tried their best to raise their children well with good hearts and a strong faith to Allah. Our late father had always been a great provider, and our mother nurtured us well. Their undying efforts have greatly influenced us, not only during our younger years but still to this day.

Patience, patience, and patience. It is not every day we will get the opportunities we want. One thing we have learned is that life will give you the platform to get an opportunity, but it is in your hands to work it out and take hold of that opportunity. There is no easy path; it takes a lot of patience and perseverance. As we started to make our choices in life, struggles were always present. Each struggle has taught us a lesson. For each mistake, we learned our lessons. Our experiences in our younger years influenced the roads we wanted to take.

Mohamed and I were born just a year apart. Our small age gap made us the closest among our siblings. We were raised almost like twins, and some people have even said that we look alike. We have the same circle of friends. Our interests are similar, but we also have differences, like all siblings. I would describe us like yin and yang. We may have some differences, but our personalities complement each other. It has made us inseparable and better together. We always look up to each other and have each other's back. That is how strong our bond has been up to the present; it has been strengthened through the years.

Mohamed is one of my older siblings; he stood like a model to me. Of course, my father will always be my first inspiration and model, but undeniably, Mohamed is one of the people I will always look up to with respect. His unstoppable determination in life truly contributed to who I am today.

Ahmed and I were very much alike in everything. We both decided to take up mechanical engineering after high school. After I finished my engineering courses, I managed to get work as a warehouse store operator for the Bahrain Petroleum Company. After working for some time, I truly wasn't satisfied with the duties I had been doing. I felt that it wasn't the career I wanted, thinking that I didn't study engineering to work in a warehouse. I decided to walk a different path. But starting out on a new journey building my career wasn't as easy as I'd imagined it would be. I faced a lot of challenges with the reality of life. Each day, I appreciate more and more the efforts of my father. I realized that I was no longer playing and that everything was real.

The treatment I received at my first job wasn't as I expected it to be. It was saddening, but instead of quitting, it pushed me to see the bright side of the challenges and improve myself. I thought since I'd already been through a lot I would just stop because I didn't have enough qualifications. One thing that I learned from my father's hardships was to never let anything define you. I often tell myself, "No matter what happens, I will keep going." Sometimes we just need to challenge ourselves rather than letting other people or situations measure us. Part of challenging myself was to admit that I needed to improve myself, so I decided to continue studying and enrolled in a bachelor's course in business information system at the University of Bahrain. Never a doubt came in my mind as to whether I could do it. All I thought was that I *must* do it. So, as the sayings goes, "no pain, no gain," so no excuses. I managed to arrange my working hours at Bahrain Petroleum Company so I could attend my classes. The sweet irony of it was that I was at the new chapter in my life building my own family—another reason to do better and to do more.

People call me crazy for doing it all at the same time. Honestly, it was so tiring and took so much of my time, but my dissatisfaction with the treatment I received had fueled my desires to improve myself for family and myself. I continued to keep going and juggling with all struggles, but none of it made me think of stopping or quitting. It was extremely difficult, but I managed to continue attending my classes while working. I strived in full swing and in God's willingness, I have completed my course and achieved my bachelor's degree half a year earlier with flying colors.

> *When you feel as though you can't do something, the simple antidote is action: Begin doing it. Start the process, even if it's just a simple step, and don't stop at the beginning.*
>
> — Marcus Buckingham

All hard work was paid for when I managed to secure a position as System Analyst and Programmer at the Bahrain Petroleum

Company. My brother and I must have too many common interests, but Ahmed seemed to developed a different interest for his future career and had a change of hearts. From Mechanical Engineering, he shifted into Sales & Marketing studies.

I wasn't the only one with a challenging life after studying. The same was true for my younger brother Ahmed. After almost a year of working in Bahrain, Ahmed decided to move to another country. He joined Infolink Consultancy with its headquarters in Abu Dhabi, United Arab Emirates, to try his luck in the field of marketing. Working abroad had widen his horizon, not only gaining experience at work but learning to socialize with other nationalities and different cultures.

With the open environment, Ahmed enjoyed working abroad, as he has his own freedom and gained a lot from the international community, both professionally and personally. Ahmed was happy with his life abroad, but despite the opportunities, he felt it was the time for him to serve his country to adapt and apply everything he had learned. The following year, he decided to resign and return home. Also, he could have been enjoying the life abroad, but he realized that he could not live far away from his home country for a long time. When he came back, he luckily managed to secure a job in a multinational company called FranklinCovey. Little did he know that it would totally change his life and himself for the better.

Huda Al-Khawaja interviewed Ahmed, and he couldn't forget that opportunity when he knew he'd been chosen not for his background but for his personality. Huda Al-Khawaja gave Ahmed a great opportunity and mentored him while working at FranklinCovey. Ahmed didn't let that chance slip through his hands and grasped it tightly. He took all the opportunities that could help him improve himself and went through trainings with *The 7 Habits of Highly Effective People* so many times he lost track.

I was impressed with Ahmed's devotion practicing it in his daily living. His mentor, Huda Al-Khawaja, wasn't only his boss but a living model to my brother, as she has shown him how to walk the talk. My brother often says that he wouldn't be where he is without the people he worked with at FranklinCovey, especially Huda Al-Khawaja.

Ahmed had been doing well at FranklinCovey, so he decided to stay in Bahrain for good and start his family. Working for a multinational company, Ahmed had the opportunity to travel in and out of Bahrain for training. His training and exposure had greatly improved his interpersonal, administrative, sales, and marketing skills. It was truly a great training ground for him to improve his professional and personal skills.

Due to the economic situation, management decided to shift their operations in Bahrain to their office in Dubai in 2002. It was another challenge to Ahmed, as he had decided to stay in Bahrain for good. However, he was not ready to leave his work, so he moved back to United Arab Emirates and joined their operations in Dubai. A few months later, Ahmed decided to end his tenure with FranklinCovey and return home. It wasn't an easy decision after having that once-in-a-lifetime opportunity to be surrounded with great people, but one thing that I admired the most with my brother is his commitment to family. After returning to Bahrain, Ahmed secured a full-time job at United Gulf Bank, an offshore bank with its office located at Diplomatic Area, Manama.

As Ahmed and I started to establish our own families and with ourselves in our chosen career paths, through our passion for volunteering, we started to explore the world of traveling. Our passion has opened our eyes to the opportunity of exploring other places. It all started as we honored and paid respect to our holy devotions. That also gave us the chance to deal with and guide people. It has been a normal practices since we were young within the Gulf Region, especially with the people from the Kingdom of Bahrain and Eastern Region of Saudi Arabia. Through friends, we manage to be part of groups as volunteers in *hamlas*, which are campaigns for Islamic pilgrimage and have been done religiously every year. It was a good learning experience to handle situations and guide people. Because we were both working full time and had families, we could only join the groups on a part-time basis.

Travel and tourism has become one of the booming industries in the Middle East as developments have been improved over the last decade. As the origin of the world's three major religions, the Middle East has been one of the leading destinations for tourists from all over the world making either religious or cultural visits. This has been the case for not only several decades but for centuries.

Bahrain has been one of the central hubs in the Gulf Region. Its tradition, culture, and people could be bound and shaped by its geography and history, but as development progresses, our society has changed too. The demand of traveling has dramatically increased from religious pilgrimages to business and employment trips. With the remarkable tourism development in the region, religious tours have been a tradition passed from generation to generation and have become a societal norm. One of the norms that has been going on every year is a group of family and friends traveling together to pay a visit to religious places such as holy shrines in honor of religious beliefs and to spiritually contemplate.

People from the Middle East are known for traveling in large groups. Locals, especially from Bahrain and Saudi Arabia, love to go in large groups with their families, as they get the chance to gather around and even meet new people on their travels. This social travel trend has influenced the majority and has become more popular in our society. Thus, those religious tours have been devotedly done and promoted annually as hamlas in the Gulf Region, mostly in Bahrain and Saudi Arabia.

Every year, a hamla is being launched and promoted everywhere in the country, wherein complete packaged tours to pilgrimages destinations such as Masjid al-Haram in Mecca, Al-Masjid an-Nabawi in Medina, and the Mada'in Saleh archaeological sites, among other sites in Saudi Arabia, Iran, Iraq, and Syria. Hamla is also known as a campaign to encourage groups of people to book their trips alongside other devotees to visit religious destinations. As the years passed, these trips became in demand, and more companies promoted hamlas all around the kingdom.

As one of the common traditions of every family in Bahrain, joining a hamla became a must for every family member once they reached the right age to participate. In 2002 for Hajj, which is the annual pilgrimage to Mecca, it was the first hamla that Mohamed joined. From that trip, Mohamed had the opportunity to use his passion of helping other people for a good cause. He enjoyed that the trip was not only to develop his spiritual beliefs but an opportunity to be of help to the elderly who joined hamla.

The next year, Mohamed traveled again for Hajj, but this time as one of the pilgrims and a volunteer to help and assist the other pilgrims. During the pilgrimage, he met an old acquaintance, Husain, who is one of our dear friends today and one of the pillars in Spring. Since then, they have joined the hamla every year as volunteers.

In 2005, I decided to join hamla and be one of the pilgrimage's volunteers. While volunteering for years, our passion for traveling outgrew us and became one of our hobbies that we both love and are eager to pursue. It is not only a chance to explore places but also gain knowledge and experiences that have impacted our deep interest and passion in widening our horizons.

Because we were both working full time and had growing families to take care of, we joined hamla on a part-time basis. Mohamed used to be group leader and facilitator, meeting every need of every member of their group. He was guiding all pilgrims to their accommodations. Ahmed and Husain were also volunteers, assisting Mohamed facilitate every pilgrim during Hajj, circling and protecting the group, especially the women. Since then, we had devotedly continued volunteering for hamlas such as Umrah and Hajj for roughly around five years. Most of the said tours that we led were Hajj in Saudi Arabia.

The Ministry of Justice and Islamic Affairs has changed the rules and policy for hamlas, wherein only licensed companies will be allowed to facilitate all pilgrimage camps. Since then, companies handling hamlas shifted to touristic tours. Slowly, as it has been continuously promoted, the demand has been increasing as well. As modern development advances, traveling has become easier and more comfortable. New airlines, new flights, new hotels, and more travel service providers started to dramatically grow in the market, which opened more options traveling to and from the Gulf Region.

In early 2007, we decided to join the same company where we used to be volunteers as part-time tour leaders promoting tourism in new travel destinations such as Turkey and the Far East, including Malaysia and Thailand. Because it was still fresh in the market, the demand of traveling in private in such touristic places was low, as well as very costly. More promotions had been launched, but the demand was still low, as the acceptance of this touristic trip was not immediate in our society. As tourism has been widely promoted, people have slowly started to accept the new traveling norms. The good economic gains in the Gulf Region was an added factor in the increase of demand, as it enhanced the spending of people on international tourism, such as the locals from the Kingdom of Bahrain and Saudi Arabia who usually travel in large groups. Visiting new tourist destinations became more common among the locals to spend their holidays going to the new destinations for recreation and leisure.

In 2010, as travel and tourism dramatically increased, we still focused on our full-time work and progressively held our key positions in our respective work commitments. In addition, we continued leading groups, and as the demands for tourism continuously increased, we started to promote European destinations. The same year, Mohamed led his first group to Europe, visiting Munich, Germany, and Salzburg, Zell am See, and Vienna, Austria. Not all first attempts are successes.

Our first European group was a failure and complete disaster. We faced a lot of problems with the bookings and arrangements during the entire trip. It was Mohamed's first time to visit Europe, and frankly, he didn't have enough clear information gathered before the trip. With all the difficulties and headaches we experienced with our first group, we were sure to note all of our errors and the issues we faced. Proper preparations, procedures, and precautions were applied in the following European groups. Additionally, we changed the process of arrangements and instead patterned the trip the same way we arranged the religious tours. It was a formula of trial and error. It worked in the following trips, which were far better than the first European group. Because it was effective, European tours were promoted at least twice a year. Since then, we have made more promotions and have been able to establish more touristic packaged groups.

In 2011, many things changed in Bahrain, but the demand in tourism was still growing, and the potential income was undeniably impressive. It had been a challenging year, and the industry had also taken much of our time because we were both working full time in our respective jobs. Juggling many hats, Mohamed had decided to follow his passion and focus mainly on the travel industry. It wasn't an easy path for him after leaving the bank and took a lot from him, such as the fixed income every month, incentives, and bonuses, but this was what motivated Mohamed to do more instead of being held back with the unstable situation of beginning his new journey while establishing himself solely in the travel industry.

Being in the industry as tour leaders for almost a decade, Mohamed and I had built our names in the market and earned our good reputation. That later provided Mohamed an opportunity to lead as a deputy chief executive officer in one of the travel agencies in Bahrain. A bigger role, more responsibilities, and new challenges came with it, along with growing demand, as more competitors were emerging in the market. Because Mohamed was the deputy CEO and had the freedom of his time, he was able to focus on getting into the market on his own platform and focused on doing promotions.

He fueled up and transitioned the company into modern management.

He built his own entourage of tour leaders and established his own accounts and clients that generated great revenue for the company. In 2012, with all his great efforts and creative strategies, Mohamed earned a respectable position and credibility in the market, and thus, he became one of the shareholders of the company. Not only that, but I was a part-time tour leader assisting and leading groups, and I had been a helping hand to him as well. I have always given my voluntary support to Mohamed in terms of business development, planning, sales, and marketing assistance, which I still do today. He is not only my brother. Even in our casual talks, I always give him my opinion to help him make better trip packages and more effective marketing, which he openly accepts and analyzes, factoring it into his management and promotions.

Mohamed, with all his efforts all through the years, had led the company to be one of the leading outbound travel agencies in Bahrain. More tours were promoted, and they were a hit every summer. As a usual stage in our lives, we face some situations that open new doors of opportunity that have been waiting for us to discover and ponder.

Like the advanced technology that has been continuously improving, we also search for our self-improvements, and those ideas usually come from the challenges we face. Hence, a new horizon comes up, and we sometimes wonder whether we can make it. It is like jumping into a cliff of wonders. Are you going to jump and explore the great feeling and adventure it could give you, or do you just want to stay still and stand at the edge of the cliff while you watch others enjoy the wonders? So, the day came when an idea struck: Why not jump off the cliff and be independent? Why not establish our own travel company. The idea was an eye-opener to a greater vision.

After hearing the idea from Ahmed, my initial reaction was that it was a drastic idea, but in the back of my mind, I am not willing to just stay inside the box and lose the chance to strike the iron while it's still hot. The travel market was booming, so I considered crackling a new journey, but it wasn't easy.

The realization of the difficulties involved starting from zero again was the first thing to be considered. I had an internal judgment about whether I could do it, so I told Ahmed to give me some time to think well about the idea. After some time, I had given my initial approval to Ahmed, but deep inside, I wasn't fully sure of my decision, so I took considerations from the opinion of our family and close friends. Sadly, the majority didn't support the idea, like the others who just want to stay still on the edge of the cliff concerning whether you'll be able to do it. I had already established myself. Why take a leap and start over again?

It was truly challenging thinking of the consequences but also getting into the process with family and friends. There have been some words thrown at me that truly hurt my feelings, but I considered that I had so many things I knew would be great and that I truly wanted to do. Still, I was always in the same corner, waiting for approval to do so. I felt like a bird kept in a cage, wanting his freedom to fly wherever he wants.

It took me a lot of thinking, and as I look back from the day my father sent me to start working with all experiences and lessons in life that I have learned, I believe that no matter what happens, I know I can do it, and it will be for the better. Like an epic horse rider, riding for years and years on the same track, the day will come when you know it is time to let go of your horse and start to walk on a different path. We all have the right to end one chapter and open a new one in our lives, so I did.

I had given my word to my brother, and I was very thankful to all our family and friends. Not all of them might have accepted our decision, but all of them gave their understanding and full support. Hasan Sabba has been one of the most supporting family members who has played a big role during the transition as our partner. He has been not only a cousin but a very dear friend to me and my brother. With all the challenges, the fun began as we partook in our new journey ... Let the new chapter begin.

Chapter 2

Plunged in Bahrain's Travel Market

The beginning is the most important part of the work.

— Plato

We trust in God and the power of our dear parents' prayers. From the heart of deprivation and poverty, our persistence was born, and so we have restored our moment and made our final decision to take a step and start our own travel and tour business. Our first journey was about to start.

Taking a step forward, we held our very first meeting between myself and my brother Mohamed to lay all ideas on the floor and brainstorm how to take our initial actions in opening our company. We had deliberated about how we could introduce our company and how we could gain access to the travel market among the established companies that already had their roots well planted in the market.

Looking at our combined experiences, there had been tons of ideas that came out. The ideas were like looking at the twigs and branches of a big, old tree. Among all the ideas, the first that came up was to change the concepts of travel and tourism to the local and other travelers within the Gulf Region. It was truly an inspiring idea and almost sounded like a fairy tale to others—but not to us. It was a challenging idea and would take tremendous effort to begin. Looking at the pros and cons, it came with too many obstacles. We didn't let the obstacles hinder us to start; instead, we used the obstacles as fuel to see how we could make things happen in reality and not just keep them as ideas or big dreams in our minds. There was a proverb that my beloved late father always told me when we were young: "When you begin to trust yourself, you are on the right path to success and progress."

We strongly believe in change … changing in concepts and customs. Sometimes, when you are already in the loop for a long time, changing the course is not easily accepted and mostly refused. How do we achieve that? We believe you must be strong-willed to pursue the changes you want to introduce, as there will be a lot of resistance coming from many places, including the people who will be most affected by the change you are instigating. The process is like sailing against the waves to reach your destination.

We are well aware that the journey will be rough, but we also know that once you reach your destination, it is the sweetest and greatest feeling that every moment will be memorable. Persistence—we vowed to keep our persistence no matter what happened and to reach our goal to bring better changes. From our teenage years, we learned from our parents and our own experiences that you must take a firm stand for the changes you desire.

Riding on the same path does not bring an improvement, but it is like running on a treadmill. No matter what your speed or how long you run or walk, you are still in the same place. We have chosen to take a ride on a road where it can lead us to different destinations. Not everyone has the courage to go against the waves, as taking that path in a different direction is a big risk to take. Either you succeed or you fail. Mohamed is a strong-willed person, and no matter what happens, he keeps going and doesn't allowing failures to get the best of him. This is a great advantage of having him leading us.

We envisioned our company like the Tree of Life—yes, the Tree of Life. It's not surreal, but it's real. It exists, and you can see it in the Kingdom of Bahrain. It is as iconic as the story it says. It was one of our inspirations of how and where we want to be in the market. As a new player in the travel and tourism industry, our start would be our marking point on where our stand in the market would be. We aimed to have our company's roots robustly founded, just like of the Tree of Life, so it could withstand the defiance of the travel industry.

Building up our strong foundation was one of the most important steps to begin. We looked into ourselves and categorized what could help us to achieve our goal. One of our main strengths is that we both strongly believe in our capabilities and our perseverance to succeed in starting and fueling up the company. We used the capabilities we had developed from our personal experiences along with thorough research of the market in order to identify what was generally available in the market and figure out how we could improve it. As part of a hamla, travelers didn't expect more than the usual services available on the market, which included booking of the airfare, hotel accommodation, and transportation arrangements—all with a lot of errors.

The travel market was already mature with many options available. Having a strong foundation doesn't guarantee getting through and not being like the usual travel company in the market. The challenge is how can we stand out and not go unnoticed? Our main perception was to be unique and feature services that were fresh and remarkable to be presented to the customers with a competitive price.

A lot of research and preparation went into starting up our company. Naming our company was one of the crucial parts of our start-up, as it would be the name customers, friends, and families would remember. We decided not to choose a name that reflected our family name, city, or any religious affiliation, so people would deal with the company itself and not due to as association with anything. It was also to keep our field open and flexible for any future expansions. We wanted our company name to stand out, stay, and keep up in the market without being associated with any individual, group, organization, institution, or establishment. After thoughtfully weighing our options, we came up with the name Spring.

It has many meanings, depending on how you want to use it, and all are positive. Spring's meaning is mostly "to come out, to arise, to grow, to develop." The world blooms in spring season, so it brings hope to people. The word itself is very encouraging, like the quote from Leo Tolstoy: "Spring is the time of plans and projects." We all agreed to name our company Spring Travel and Tourism, as it was perfect for what we aimed for our company to be.

I am extremely proud of my brother, Ahmed. Since our younger years, he has never failed to amaze me with his eminent creativity. His boundless imagination was truly an asset in our creative marketing from the beginning and still is today. In addition to his natural creative talent, he has a great marketing background that truly helped us in forming our advertisements and promotions.

After finalizing our company name, we started our branding, which was headed by Ahmed himself. We chose a color that perfectly reflects Spring—a green apple shade. It was a different from what was commonly available and used in the market. Most travel companies, including the airlines and hotels, were using red, blue, and orange, which sometimes makes it hard to differentiate them. We chose the green apple color for our logo and our entire branding, as the color reflects nature, freshness, calming, peace, and relaxation, making Spring Travel the only travel company with a unique color. The color itself helped identify Spring Travel as striking out in the open field.

After creating our identity, we focused on the services that we wanted to offer in the market that were different from what was already in the industry. We wanted to come out and stick to our concept of being an exclusive company offering unique services. It was the trademark we wanted every person to know and remember about us.

We explored ideas for a long time and came up with an innovative way of organizing tour groups. Travelers would be fully aware of all related information before even registering for a trip. This would include the airline, flight times, tour captains, daily tour program, hotel and accommodation plan, rights and duties of the traveler, other included services, optional services, and so on. Services that were not included in the offer were also explained well. This has been one of the important parts of the process in the industry that had been mostly neglected—or rather misquoted—for the travelers. This part of the process is where many inconveniences cause problems to either the tour company or the travelers themselves, and sometimes issues are encountered by both parties. Tour organizing is not just putting the trip together. We add our personal touch, which is one thing no one can copy. Our personal touch is one of the most unique ways we can provide our services to the customers.

Being different and unique is not enough unless we have an outstanding marketing plan that can spread out all our ideas properly. Ahmed's exposure in textile industry during his younger years had made him interested in sales and marketing, and he even took a college course to enrich his knowledge. I would say Ahmed is a very clever person, not because he is my brother but because one of his strengths is his strategy in marketing. I believe his early exposure truly helped him, and it became an addition to our advantage, which we consider one of our building tools that we hardly worked on.

The idea of marketing seemed easy and can be when an outsource firm is used, but we put our own efforts in it to make sure that our ideas were imprinted on each strategy we envisioned. Our marketing plan was strengthened by its main axes, such as indirect advertising, social contribution, and investment in human resources.

The adoption of indirect marketing methods did not yet exist in the travel market industry. Creating promotions is easy as long as you have the money to fund them, but you have to work on a promotion that will connect you to people. Otherwise, your efforts will end up wasted in promoting with no audience. We have chosen indirect marketing, as we believe in the impact it makes in the market and to the people. It is not only promotions but also spreading stories that will help us build a connection with everyone. We wanted to communicate and relate to each person we were trying to reach.

As we built our company, it was and always will be of great importance for Spring Travel to be part of the community and have an impact in our customers' lives as much as possible. One of our goals was to make Spring Travel part of special times in our customers' lives in a way that we will always be remembered aside from the great memory of the trip they took with us.

We were keen on establishing a deep connection with our customers, as it was one of best leverages in our success. Every customer, our travelers, and their happiness are part of our success. Helping them reach their dream destinations is part of us encouraging each one of them to pursue their travel plans and make memories of a lifetime. We put our utmost pleasure in arranging and organizing each trip, as if it were our own trip. Relating to each one of our customers gives us the edge of connecting easily and establishing a good rapport.

Additionally, we started looking at the common interests of the community, such as cultural, sports, and community events, in addition to Ramadan competitions. We wanted to encourage and inspire future generations to believe they could make their dreams come true with perseverance and motivation.

From our humble beginnings, we always look back to honor our roots, which helped us reach our current standing in life and who we are now. In addition to building connections, we wanted to give our utmost support to the community. As part of the community, we believe that we all have social participation. Part of our mission is that Spring Travel will be an establishment that contributes to social awareness of community initiatives, such as cancer awareness, national celebrations, global campaigns, and various religious occasions.

Moreover, Spring Travel is committed to honor students, our future generation, who are exemplary and excelling in academics to give them commendations and encouragement to keep up their good work. We believe in each one of them to be our rising generation of future leaders.

Our mission and the vision for our company had been laid out, and we needed to build and materialize it. We could have the best ideas, plans, and strategies, but how could we make those things happen? We needed good people who could be our helping hands as we strove to achieve our goals. The travel market was like joining a running competition. We needed a strong and good runner to win the race.

One of the main keys to the success of our plans and marketing strategies was relying in a great investment in human resources. We not only needed to find good team members but build our team to be enabled to relive our mission and vision. Our team is one of our main assets, and we strive to empower them with proper knowledge and give them the resources they need to perform their tasks. All staff would be well equipped when we started operating. Our staff would not just be employees but family.

We wanted to build a family within Spring Travel that later would grow into a community. Each staff member would be appreciated, as every effort counted as we made our path into success. It's like counting; one million will never be one million without one.

Our parents taught us to value everything whether big or small—it all matters. We must appreciate and be grateful for everything. With our credibility in the market as individuals, as Mohamed Al Hamad and Ahmed Al Hamad, finding staff for Spring Travel was easy, but the selection was the tricky part of it. We made a set of criteria to help us select members of our team. It was one of the hardest tasks either of us had ever done, as we needed to find the right team members to fill the required positions with the same level of enthusiasm as we had.

We found many talented people from recommendations, old acquaintances, industry connections, and good friends. We had to prioritize selecting our frontline workers, tour leaders, and members of the office sales staff. Ahmed handled most of the recruitment process, but we both selected the final candidates.

Two heads are better than one.

— John Heywood

Zainab Al Durazi is one of our pioneer team members we hired to join our sales team, and she is happily part of our growing family. We strongly believed in the English proverb, "Two heads are better than one." Hence, as a travel company, our doors are always open to other nationalities because we believe they are great addition and will make a great contribution to the diversity of our operations and work culture. We have confidence that having different nationalities in our workplace will bring a healthy environment, so we have hired team members from other nations like India, Nepal, Indonesia, and the Philippines. We have set things up so that all tour leaders are Bahrainis, as it is easier to have someone who understands the common tongue and shares the same culture.

Our ideologies had been formed, and it was time to find a good home for our company. We considered that it would not only be our home base but one of our main visible selling points. We scouted a lot of places and narrowed it down to nearby places till we chose Budaiya, mainly because of the population and accessibility. The area was easily accessible for our customers. Luckily, Gardens Plaza had just opened for rent and was strategically located along the highway. In addition, Spring would be the only travel service provider within the mall.

Ahmed, being keen on details, helped quite a lot to align our projections specifically with our marketing. We managed to apply our branding well not only with our promotion materials but down to the smallest details in our office, such as the stationery. We noticed that none of our competitors had ever been into branding with a unified theme—from office interiors to the smallest details of their operations. Spring's branding had created a model—one line of movement that people could easily recognize and tell that it was Spring.

We aimed to have the prestige of being consistent in most of what we do and what we show to people, as it would be an evident example for each traveler to see that we have specific standards for how we organize and do things. We strive to provide an excellent quality of services to each customer.

Our branding started from the design of our office interior. The main concept was to showcase our color motif—green apple—in a sleek design, giving it an ambiance of a stylish, clean, posh look. We made a good investment and sound efforts building our office, as it was phase one of our main sales pipeline. We made thorough preparations, not to show to people who visit that we have a great interiors but to show how we get into details. It would definitely give them an idea of the kind of services we could offer them. Some may consider this showing off, but our intention has always been to give each person who steps into our office a picture of how determined and serious we are in our commitment to excellence and high standards.

After the interior was complete, our office would not be an office without our dedicated team—our office members and tour captains. Our team would become one of our major assets and serve as our models. They would carry out our branding and, most importantly serve as helping hands to achieve our mission and reach our vision.

From our first brainstorming period, we set things up so each member would be provided all the resources in alignment with our plans. We built a distinct identity to give them the feeling of prestige working with us and to be part of our family and the community we wanted to build. Part of our goal was to create a great perspective with every staff and give them a sense of belonging. Providing each staff member with uniforms is not only part of our branding, but it gives them an affirmation that they are one of us—part of the Spring family. Our staff uniform was delicately designed to carry out the smart image we wanted them to have—elegant, stylish, professional, and highly respectable. We personally believe that when you look good, you feel good too.

Designing the image of our team members was one of the best times we had during planning stage. It gave us a great feeling seeing that we had created something. It was fun seeing how they would look and especially the idea of how each one of them would proudly wear it. It also gave us a great feeling of achievement and encouragement. Aside from glamming up, the comfort of our team members was of essence. We designed their dedicated areas to be comfortable so that working would be cozy and enjoyable. We have always aimed to provide our team a happy workplace that allows them to have a great environment and creates an invigorating culture.

We also work to empower each staff member to become confident in everything they do, whether for Spring or for personal enjoyment. To complete their smart package, we planned a series of trainings and seminars for our members that would help them become knowledgeable and master their expertise in handling all inquiries and bookings.

The success of our groups would rely mostly on our tour captains, as they would be the ones to lead groups during trips. In line with that idea, we determined that each tour captain would be given mandatory and necessary training, especially regarding how to handle sensitive situations like emergencies cases. The safety of every person traveling with us of our utmost concern.

As the leaders of our team, we ensure all members are well trained and have the capacity to manage all possible scenarios—from booking through the trip itself. The readiness of our team members is one of the best ways for us to ensure smooth operations. Admirably, it helps us to gain and build the trust of our customers, as they see that we know what we are doing.

Having said so, supporting and empowering each of our team members is part of the steps we take to build a good culture for our Spring community. Seeing them succeed in every task they do will be our success too. We believe that bolstering our staff will encourage them to do better and more than they could imagine. We want to motivate them to open their horizons to all possibilities—the same attitude we have. It also adds prestige to our team when people can distinguish them from the rest of the market. Not only do we want to impress our own team, but we want others to be impressed with the level of professionalism and overall package each member of our team showcases to the public. We aspire to promote a great environment at our workplace for each talented member, which will also attract others to be part of our team.

Our branding pipeline doesn't only cover our marketing and operations but also the people who will be traveling with us. We have designed things so our groups will be easily identified by our tour captains. We give away some gifts that they can use while traveling. These travel accessories help us identify who is traveling with us, helping our tour captains locate each traveler among the crowd. We are glad that the color itself has made an impact on people from Bahrain and the Eastern province of the Kingdom of Saudi Arabia, green apple is known for Spring Travel.

The usual forms of marketing for most companies include sending bulk SMS text messages or leaflets through the post office to be distributed with every electric and water bill. As a newcomer in the market, we don't want to start using common marketing tactics.

We introduced our group packages with a tour packages guide. Ahmed's background in doing conference and exhibition catalogues helped in making our annual tour packages' guide for every summer season filled with useful information that every traveler needs know, including the weather forecast, currency exchange, things to do, visa requirements, real photos, embassy and consulate contact details, check-in and airport instructions, plus our company profile.

Our portfolio was finally completed and fully ready to showcase our exciting services to the market. Because I was still finishing some engagements and Ahmed was preparing for our own groups, we started offering private tours. The booking inquiries we received were truly heartwarming, and it added more enthusiasm for our group packages. Sometimes we joked to some friends: "Oh well. We cannot sleep till we start launching our packages."

The thrill of our new journey began when we announced our first group to Turkey for *Eid al-Adha*. Our phone lines rang around the clock with lots of inquiries, as most people could not believe the price and inclusions of our packages. Our very first package was a sprint and sold like hotcakes.

There were a great number of people who knew our reputation, but there were some people who called to check every detail, as they found our package unbelievable. That's why Ahmed and I personally attended to inquiries and assisted every customer asking about our package. We were surprised by the incredible response we received from the market. It was what we had dreamed about. Our group was already full, but we kept receiving inquiries. People wanted to be added to the group, but we could not take more. We could have accepted a lot of bookings, but we didn't want to compromise the quality of our service. We wanted to make sure that every person who traveled with our first group was well attended to.

Our first group was personally handled and led by Ahmed. My brother might have had the experiences, but knowing that it was his first time to be in Turkey, I truly admired his courage for accepting the challenge to lead our very first group. During our younger years, we both developed this attitude of striving to always be the first, allowing ourselves to do and be better. It may have been a challenge to Ahmed, but with the prestige of handling our first group, there was nothing that would let his spirit down. He may not have been fully familiar with place, but he did his best handling our group.

He woke up early to prepare for the group and make sure that everyone was well prepared to set out for the tour. He planned out the tour, making sure our group was always the first to arrive at the tour destinations. This allowed our group to maximize the opportunity of privacy before places became too crowded. Ahmed is truly a comical person, and this was an added advantage while handling our group. There were no dull moments, as he got every member of our group to sing with him while on the tour and other entertainment that everyone enjoyed—even the little ones.

I was amazed that Ahmed did his homework well and packed an extra personal surprise for our group. Because it was Eid al-Fitr, the little ones enjoyed receiving *eidya* (Money, gift, candy, and others given to children on the occasion of Eid), and he distributed a delicious baklava from Mado to our group and fellow Bahraini groups that they met at the hotel. It was just a kind gesture from him, as he believed that sharing was caring. His packed surprises for our group didn't end there, as during the Bosporus cruise, he brought a surprise cake for our group to enjoy and shared it with everyone on board.

When our group returned to Bahrain, everyone had developed a great bond with the other families they traveled with, and everyone came home with smiles on their faces. It was a massive success for our very first group, and the feedback from each traveler was truly heartwarming.

In the beginning of our launch, our competitors were confident that we would not do well with our group packages. Instead, our first package sparked a boiling point among competitors in the market, which raised eyebrows and teased them into a melting pot. Because our first launch caused a stir, there were some people who tried to manipulate the market to create a fuss about us.

Business was indeed a monopoly, and we expected such things to happen. We aimed to bring change to the industry, and we knew not everyone would be pleased. Our grand entrance had gained too much attention, and some competitors were not happy with it. Some had doubted us, as if we were just a gimmick. But when our travelers came back and started to share their experiences, the noise of our name became louder and louder. It wasn't only the travelers who had joined our group talking, but others who had witnessed how great our group was also gave us great feedback and checked out our services.

Resistance to change is always the biggest obstacle.

— Chris Paine

It caused such a stir that some competitors even united in an effort to take Spring Travel out of the market. They have tried to stop us from establishing our stand in the market and build our business. We were thrilled to see that our marketing plan and all preparations were effective and worked out well. We faced the initial challenges, and we maintained our investments in our marketing, keeping ourselves on the ground. There were businesses that wouldn't gamble to reduce their profit, but we believed that reducing our profit margin was one of our strongest investments, as not all competitors would dare to do the same because they were used to very high profit margins and definitely wanted to keep things as they were.

One of the life lessons we both learned from our beloved parents was to be genuinely generous, and everything will come in a hundredfold. From the benefit of enjoying our passion of traveling, we can share and help travelers by taking take them to their dream destinations. We give our heart and passion by doing this business and offer every traveler an innovative option.

We are grateful for every person who stood and supported our first launch even if there were some people who tried to break the wheel of progress. Our first group was indeed a hit with the help and enormous support of our beloved parents, families, friends, and great team, as well as our travelers who were impressed and trusted us all the way. Spring Travel entered the market in a good standing to become one of the leading travel companies in a relatively short time.

Chapter 3

Spring and Bahrain's Travel Trend

*It's only after you've stepped outside your comfort
zone that you begin to change, grow, and transform.*

— Roy T. Bennett

Recalling our first meeting, one of the ideas that came up was changing the concept of travel and tourism for the travelers themselves.

The Bahrain travel market is a very conservative, yet I would say it's been a curious market since it opened its doors to the world. With the people from different nations who helped build the development of all industries in the Kingdom of Bahrain and other nearby Gulf countries, the culture and behavior of the Gulf people have changed and developed too.

As we say, change is indeed the only permanent thing in the world. Also, we believe that progress is the one of the constant things in our lives. We grow, we develop, we age, we mature, and, eventually, we get old. The development of our country has been so progressive and truly improved, and so has the travel and tourism industry. Locals have started to evolve and opened their doors to visiting other countries aside from the known religious sites that most Gulf people have been visiting. Airports, hotels, and other transportation facilities within the Gulf have been developed within the last decade. Many airlines and hotels were built, which contributed to the rapid increase of demand in tourism, not only during high seasons but throughout the year. With the great number of expatriates, the culture and trends have been changed and cultivated to better ones. Locals started to visit countries from the stories they have heard.

This change in trends did not happen overnight, as the colloquial response from the locals themselves. For locals, traveling is a yearly must in order to pay respects to religious sites commemorating our devotion to the history of our religion and beliefs. People would save funds to join pilgrimage camps in Saudi Arabia, Iran, Iraq, and Syria. But in in the mid-2000s, due to the government's change of policies and rules for such pilgrimages, most of the travel companies switched and promoted touristic trips. It was something new in the market to spend vacation for relaxation instead of joining religious camps, which was not easily accepted by the locals.

Normally, the locals would spend money on religious visit rather than touristic trips, as religious trips were seen as worthy of every penny. Touristic trips were accepted gradually, and it took years to be fully accepted in our society.

I remember sometime in 2015 we still had friends who were not telling their family and friends that they were traveling to such touristic destinations like Far East Asia. It was still a debate to the majority of the locals whether they should travel in countries other than those that housed common destinations for religious visit. Because a lot of companies began promoting touristic trips, it was slowly accepted by the locals in Bahrain and other nearby countries in the Gulf.

As the years have passed, the number of travelers has dramatically increased. One of the main reasons is the effect of the expatriates living in the Gulf. Expatriates helped by not only bringing in and building the developments of our country but by contributing to the knowledge of the locals through sharing their cultures and stories about their countries. There have been a great number of expatriates from Europe, the United States,

Africa, and, of course, Asia living in Bahrain and nearby countries in the Middle East. The increased number of expatriates in the Middle East has also opened doors to more development of the travel industry.

In the Middle East, Bahrain's flag carrier, Gulf Air, was known to be one of the oldest airlines established and founded having its main hub in Muharraq, Bahrain. Due to the increasing demand of the travel industry, there have been a lot of good airlines flying in and out of the region, including Etihad Airways, Emirates, Oman Air, Saudi Arabian Airlines, and Jazeera Airways, as well as other airlines coming from different countries outside Middle East and the private charter flights.

With all the sprouting airlines within the Gulf Region taking people to many places, traveling for both locals and expatriates has become more accessible and cheaper. Alongside the airlines and hotels, many travel agencies have sprouted and begun promoting touristic trips in addition to religious campaigns, or hamlas.

Mohamed and I have been in the travel industry since our teenage years as volunteers and then part-time tour guides. Being exposed early, we have seen and experienced the roller-coaster rides of touring. Planning and arranging a tour, whether it's a religious campaign or a touristic trips, hasn't been easy, as we cannot please everyone. It is a tricky job.

Arranging a tour is not like playing with building blocks where you pile them together, put your creation in a corner, and that's it. A tour requires a lot of planning and organizing. There have been a lot of tour companies arranging hamlas, and not all were perfectly arranged.

In each tour we've planned, Mohamed and I have learned that there are a lot of things that can happen in one trip. During our volunteering years, we learned many ways to make arrangements. Also, we have seen where problems originate. Each trip we have assisted on has given us a clear picture and ideas about how things can be done on a trip. Our years of volunteering have opened our eyes to our passion for traveling and how to plan trips better. The early years of experiences have prepared and built us to be tour leaders.

Leading a group is undeniably fun and exciting, especially when you do it with a passion. Admittedly, it sounds easy, but it never is, especially when things are out of your hands. It is not only a group of people but families traveling with you. You don't only lead them but guide them within the trip. You must be ready to answer their questions. You must be able to explain how and where things are done. In addition to experience, leading a group requires a lot of patience and sound knowledge. Leadership skills are a must, as that is your best leverage to handle and take care of the group well.

It sounds like a lot, but I strongly believe that you must have the passion for traveling to be a good tour leader. Without passion, you won't be able to do it well. Having the passion will help you guide each member of your group with a smile on your face even if it's taking a lot from you. You will not feel like it is a job you do only to earn a paycheck, but you find joy guiding each member of your group on every trip. People will feel your genuine assistance, which will leave them with great memories and smiles on their faces. Members of the group will feel more confident and relaxed, knowing that they have someone with them they can count on for anything. It is not only the place that they will remember but also you—the tour leader. You become a great part of their memories. Our passion for traveling has greatly helped us connect with people.

Language is one of the biggest barriers for the travelers in Bahrain when considering where to visit. Nearby countries within the Gulf have been always preferred because we all shared the same language. Even with the enormous presence of expatriates in Bahrain, the locals are still not confident to speak in a different language, such as English, which is the common language spoken internationally.

Why did hamlas became popular, and why were people encouraged to travel that way? One of the reasons was that there's a tour guide, or tour leader, who speaks the common tongue so travelers can ask questions even if it was an Arabic-speaking country. Language is important. It is the common way we can understand each other. And when people are new to a place, they are more comfortable talking to others who speak their native language, as they understand the way they speak.

Language is also the first thing we consider when deciding how to trust another person and be confident exploring the place where we are traveling. There are some countries where even though we speak the same language, certain words have different meanings. Bahrainis and some Gulf travelers feel more comfortable with people they can speak to without thinking that they might be misunderstood.

Our culture affected the behavior of the locals, making us conservative. One of the things we considered to gain the trust of travelers was to provide them superb comfort and confidence; therefore, we have decided that our tour captains will be Bahrainis. Being travelers ourselves helped us figure out how to address the possible concerns of our travelers. We have taken measures accordingly.

> *If you want to excel in any endeavour you must pay attention to detail, know exactly what you want, have the detail on how you want it done and how you will get it done. You must realize the importance of definitions and love defining things in your life and about your life—Define your mission, define your problem, define your future, define your path and the finer details of your vision. Use your sense of imagination and creativity.*
>
> — Archibald Marwizi, *Making Success Deliberate*

Sometimes, people are not confident enough to join groups, as they are thinking there will be other people whom they don't know. In every tour, our aim is to connect every member of our group to us and to their fellow travelers. Our tour programs are designed to help our tour captains connect with each traveler.

As the travelers are getting familiar with the tour captain, the feeling of comfort and confidence starts. Our tour programs are specifically designed to help our tour captain create a camaraderie within the group as he introduces fellow travelers. Each traveler becomes confident to interact and starts to know their fellow travelers. After getting to know each other, the connection will grow and turn into bonding.

Because we understood their needs during travel, we also designed our tours to build bonds between travelers, creating a closer connection. That connection creates a strong feeling of trust and comfort, so the people on our tours no longer feel they are traveling with strangers. Instead, it is a feeling of friendship and family. It became a tradition with our groups to say that they started the tour as strangers traveling together and returned as a group of friends. The bond and connection formed with all our travelers is undeniably one of the reasons many families keep traveling with us. We believe that our groups helped people to be encouraged to travel more often.

Traveling is extremely popular, and the demand is promising. Planning a trip is one of the most stressful things to do. Yes, it is fun to travel, but planning is often a headache. This is why travel companies exist—to help every traveler lessen the hassle of planning trips.

Especially in these days, there are many companies out there that can arrange your trip. But what makes us outshine all the others in the market is that our groups have an identity that many would want to experience. Our group packages are well planned from the time you make the purchase to the end of the trip.

We are proud to say that the style of our leaflets is the best in the market. We chose to have our own packages guide that is not yet used by others in the market. We came up with the idea to introduce our first summer travel packages tour guide. Our tour guide outlines the details of the trip, and every traveler is aware of the details of the trip. We prepare our packages tour guide not only to showcase the trips we sell but to share helpful information with travelers, such as weather forecast to help them pack the proper clothing for the places they will be visiting.

Our summer packages tour guide is packed with interesting and informative details about the countries we are promoting and is filled with wonderful photos that will encourage people to visit those places. We include information about traveling guidelines that would be helpful to travelers, especially families traveling with their little ones. We put our efforts in designing our summer packages tour guide to showcase destinations and make it easier for customers to decide which trip they will be booking rather than looking at too many options.

We couldn't agree more with the inspirational quote by Walt Disney: "We keep moving forward, opening new doors, and doing new things, because we're curious and curiosity keeps leading us down new paths." Since the beginning, we aimed to bring change for improvement. Traveling is a continuous learning experience. It opens you to different worlds, different cultures, and different people.

Our summer packages tour guide not only describes the tour packages we want to sell to people. We aim for it to be a good read for every person who has a copy. We study and carefully select all content to make sure we can share necessary and interesting information to our travelers. We put our hearts into preparing it. Our packages tour guide is one of our yearly guides of activities and our milestone as well.

Successful organizing is based on the recognition that

people get organized because they, too, have a vision.

— Paul Wellstone

While we were starting up, we prepared our marketing plan and knew it would bring improvements and new strategies to the market. Part of it is empowering not only our company but every member of our team. Our groups are handled by our tour captains, who we carefully selected. Bringing them onto our team is entrusting them to be representatives for our company. Given this concept, we arrange a yearly photoshoot for our tour captains, and we use their photos in our marketing. It became the talk of the town, as no other companies did the same. It could be considered risky because staff might leave after becoming well-known.

We believe that we are giving our tour guides an opportunity, not just to be part of our team but to do great, as people will get to know them. It is always up to the individual whether he wants to be known in such a way. We can say that we are confident none of our tour captains would let the opportunity slip away.

We also publish their photographs to show them that we believe and trust them. We want every tour captain to feel that he is appreciated and that we are proud having him on our team. Because of this, we are confident that none of the worries of our friends will happen.

Alhamdulilah (praise be to God), as of today, our pool of tour captains has grown larger in a short span of time. Having them as part of our advertisements also boosted the trust of our travelers. This is one of the important concerns of people traveling with them. They are concerned whether the person they are traveling with is trustworthy. Seeing a photo will give them an internal comfort, as they will not be just accompanied by a stranger but by a well-trained tour captain. It gives them confidence, and they feel free to travel.

Our travelers always return with smiles on their faces. Why? One of the reasons is that each trip is researched, and we share our own experiences. We make sure that all travelers are informed about what they will do and see. We don't take our travelers on trips blind. During the booking period, we give them details about the trips that they are booking, and everything is followed through by our tour captains before they travel.

The tour captain introduces himself to every traveler of his group and tries his best to respond to every question. Our tour captains are of great capacity to handle queries and address every traveler's concerns before traveling. All communications are prepared according to our procedures, and all are monitored to make sure that every concern is attended to and taken care of. Our tour captains are on the front lines, as they are handling our travelers directly.

In preparation to every trip, we make sure that they are well equipped not only with their traveling gears but with necessary trainings. Every year we gather them all for a seminar and training to make sure they are aware of the latest information about the countries they are visiting.

Also, security and safety of our groups is our main priority. Every tour captain is trained to handle emergency situations or any situation that concerns the health and safety of a traveler. Additionally, each one of them is trained to communicate properly with full respect to every traveler. Given the total care package, it is one of the things we are proud of regarding our tour captains, as they also ensure they deliver great service to every traveler in their group. We are delighted with the feedback we receive from travelers, and we commend and salute them all for their great job done.

Bahrain's travel trend has been progressing and becoming more open to new destinations as the years go by. We have been in the industry of handling religious pilgrimages until more travel companies shifted to tourism due to the government's strict requirements to conduct and handle pilgrimages. Over the las half decade, we have endeavored to be part things and contribute to the progress of the travel trend within the country.

We contributed by bringing groups to different countries that are new in the market. Arranging tours is truly demanding in terms of preparation and execution. Our advertisements have taken a fair share in the market, allowing travelers to gather necessary information. This not only helps the travelers arrange their travel plans but helps us with the booking arrangements in a worry-free way. We plan our advertisements early, which enables us to make booking arrangements properly. Planning ahead of time enables us to provide quality service at great offer available in the market. The travel information we provide becomes handy for travelers and saves them from spending huge amounts of money in last minute-surcharges for arrangements and bookings. We also designed our packages for the value of every penny that they will spend for the trip at a superb comfort. Each year, we work on creating our blue ocean to work in so we can provide innovative services to our travelers.

Aside from providing our services, we believed that we had created a good platform to contribute to our society. We established Spring Travel not only to be a travel company but to be part of the community. We want to give our participation in initiatives to connect people from different families and origins. By being part of the community, we believe we have a responsibility to help those in need. As our business is progressing, we are actively engaged in community efforts and initiatives, such as contributing to spreading awareness of community campaigns.

Family is a fundamental part of our society; they are our hidden treasure and source of our happiness. Family is one of the most wonderful parts of our lives. It is too broad to define, as there are a lot of ways people give meaning to it. One of our long-term goals is to relate with every family in our society to understand what cultivates and unites them to create a great community.

We take our own family to socialize and participate in community activities, such as family day, fun run, and celebration events wherein families get a chance to meet other families and their children get to play with the other children. We want to be a helping hand for our people to encourage them to socialize and share their participation in our community. We are delighted to see when people get to know other people; their network grows and so our community grows as well.

Back in March 2017, we held our very first family day and exhibition, which was attended by many families. It was one of the most magical days we've had since we opened Spring Travel. We were delighted with the high spirits of the children playing, and listening to their laughter filled our hearts. In addition to different games, we had face painting, which the little ones loved. It wasn't only a day for kids and for parents to just be present and look after them. It was also a day when parents showcased their great talents in painting.

We had Mickey Mouse there, which got the attention of the kids and helped us entertain every guest. Our tour captains were also present and hosted the event. The event wouldn't have been complete without prizes given to the winners and also some memorable giveaways for everyone who happily participated with us. We ended the event with a cake for everyone to share as we celebrated the day. Indeed, a fun family day was had by all of us.

We also supported our government's activities like the Bahrain Sports Day, which reminds everyone to take care of their physical health. We strongly believe and support the famous tagline: "A family that runs together, stays healthy together." It became a yearly tradition for us together with all team members and tour captains to bring our families together for a fun run within Bahrain Fort at Qal'at al-Bahrain. It is a not only a day of gathering but a day to remember that we have to take care of ourselves and be physically active.

Through our groups and activities, our family gets bigger and bigger. Sometimes when people join us, whether on trips or at other events, they get to know other people and create a good connection with each other. Sometimes, while still on a trip with us, people begin talking about booking their next trip together.

We are truly fascinated with the community being developed in our groups. It is amazing! We have both led some group tours, and we have witnessed how the close bond develops with our travelers. We have seen when they arrive at Bahrain

International Airport and take a long time to bid farewell before leaving the airport to return home. It's too sweet to watch, and the feeling of being part of creating good relationships between our travelers is incredible. It is certainly priceless and one thing that we will forever treasure in our hearts.

> *I don't think quantity time is as special as quality time with your family."*

— Reba McEntire

In 2018, one of our frequent travelers told us about the children confined at Salmaniya Medical Complex who were suffering from cancer. We paid a surprise visit to those children. Our hearts and prayers are always with them as they strongly battle their devastating illness. Children are gift from God, and they are supposed to enjoy life, but there are some children who unfortunately suffer and don't deserve it. The privilege of bringing some comfort to those children meant a lot to us, as we know that our short visit to them gave them a few moments to be relieved and cheered up. Also, we gave them some token to recognize their courage to keep fighting. It was indeed heartwarming to see that we were able to make them genuinely smile and see glowing hope in their eyes through the attention we had given them.

Women are the largest untapped reservoir of talent in the world.

— Hillary Clinton

Women are one of the most essential pillars of our community. We look up to them, as they are not just women but strong human beings helping our community and society improve, starting with being mothers who take care of their children well. Admittedly, women played one of the major roles in our lives, and none of us would be in our current positions without them.

In support of the women, we yearly appreciate them by celebrating Women's Day, and we participate in breast cancer awareness. Additionally, we believe in giving women equal opportunities, so our doors at Spring Travel are always open to women who want to work with us. From the beginning, we have been employing women as part of our Spring office support staff; their organizing skills are truly admirable. Also, we have given them the chance to be tour captains, making Spring Travel the first travel company to employ women to lead our group tours, as we believe in their strength and great abilities to handle groups well.

Our company is also actively participating in community initiatives like environmental awareness. In 2019, we participated in a beach cleanup together with our team, our families, and our travelers. Climate change and global warming are affecting not only humans but all living things in the world. One of the factors that affected the worsening effects is the improper disposal of trash. We brought our children to open their eyes to the negative effects of trash not being disposed of properly and how it affects our daily lives. We also engage our children in such activities. They are becoming aware of their actions and their responsibilities in our surroundings. It was a fun morning walking along the beach shore while collecting plastic and other trash that had washed ashore. We personally like to engage in such events because it gives us an opportunity to socialize, to contribute to preserving our environment, and to learn at the same time.

Spring Travel has become a stage for us to curate and achieve our vision as individuals. Our experiences helped us to think and bring improvements not only in the business but as things apply to our daily lives. It wasn't an easy road of challenges, but the challenges brought changes for betterment. The opportunities we received and keep receiving allow us to do more and give more, which we genuinely appreciate.

The idea of bringing and taking this business is to share our visions and upgrade the services available in the market, which will benefit more people. Still today, we keep striving to find ways to contribute and bring improvement not only for us but to everyone.

We do our best to provide excellent services, and we care about your satisfaction with all of our services. We aim to be part of your lives and your great travel memories.

We aimed to bring improvements and new things to the industry, and yes, we did. We dreamed to create our own Spring community, and today, it is amazing to witness the constant support and good relations built. It gave us the confidence to claim that we have already created Spring community. So, we say: yes, we can!

Ahmed Al Hamad leading one of our group in 2017.

Springers in a fun run for a Breast Cancer Awareness campaign.

<INSERT Photo3.jpg>

Mr. Springer's birthday, 2019.

<INSERT Photo4.jpg>

Our souls are healed and enlightened by being with children.

<INSERT Photo5.jpg>

Social activities with families.

<INSERT Photo6.jpg>

The best way to cheer up yourself is to try to cheer someone else up.

<INSERT Photo7.jpg>

Springers' fun run for Bahrain Sport Day, 2019.

<INSERT Photo8.jpg>

Our tour captains celebrating Mr. Springer's Birthday, 2019.

<INSERT Photo9.jpg>

Our tour captains posing at their Istanbul Incentive Trip, 2017.

<INSERT Photo10.jpg>

"Teamwork is the ability to work together towards a common vision." —Andrew Carnegie

<INSERT Photo11.jpg>

"If it doesn't challenge you, it doesn't change you." — Fred DeVito

<INSERT Photo12.jpg>

"Never stop learning, because life never stops teaching."

<INSERT Photo13.jpg>

"Activity leads to productivity." — Jim Rohn

<INSERT Photo14.jpg>

Springers' sports activity gathering.

<INSERT Photo15.jpg>

"Don't travel just to see …"

<INSERT Photo16.jpg>

Our tour captains in one of our interesting adventures during their incentive trip, 2017.

<INSERT Photo17.jpg>

Our tour captains enjoying the lovely scenery and nature's wonders during one of our incentive trips.

Springers' Support Team at Bahrain International Airport.

"None of us is as smart as all of us." — Kenneth Blanchard

"The strength of the team is each individual member. The strength of each member is the team." — Phil Jackson

The Spring team, 2015.

<INSERT Photo22.jpg>

Management and tour captains at the end of the summer season, 2018.

<INSERT Photo23.jpg>

Spring staff members at the closing ceremony of the summer season, 2018.

<INSERT Photo24.jpg>

Spring Creative Team, 2018.

<INSERT Photo25.jpg>

Al-Ahsa branch in Kingdom of Saudi Arabia official opening, 2018.

<INSERT Photo26.jpg>

Qatif branch in Kingdom of Saudi Arabia official opening, 2019.

<INSERT Photo27.jpg>

Our tour captain send-off for our Antarctica Adventure Team.

<INSERT Photo28.jpg>

Mohamed Al Hamad and Omar Farooq, well-known social media influencer and videographer, proudly raised our Bahrain flag as they landed in Antarctica.

<INSERT Photo29.jpg>

Ahmed Al Hamad honored by Turkish Airlines, Bahrain.

<INSERT Photo30.jpg>

Mohamed and Ahmed Al Hamad with the Turkish Airlines
Team.

<INSERT Photo31.jpg>

Our new office opening, 2020. Honored by representative from
Bahrain Tourism and Exhibitions Authority, Airlines, and
Partners.

<INSERT Photo32.jpg>

Honored by the representative of Bahrain Tourism and
Exhibitions Authority during our new office opening, 2020.

<INSERT Photo33.jpg>

Spring staff during our official opening of our new premises, 2020.

<INSERT Photo34.jpg>

Our tour captains during the official opening of our new premises, 2020.

<INSERT Photo35.jpg>

<INSERT Photo36.jpg>

<INSERT Photo37.jpg>

Mr. Springer "The icon that represents Spring Travel"

Chapter 4

We Don't Follow; We Lead

Curiosity is the engine of achievement.

— *Sir Ken Robinson*

One of our goals is to bring new ideas. We challenge ourselves to come up with fresh ideas to be able to offer creativity to travelers. New ideas are products of a curious mind. You start to go in a direction that no one walks. You wonder what it could do or what it could have waiting for you. Our curiosity has led us to open our minds to look for unique strategies that can bring improvements to the market.

Some people may find it a waste of time, but nothing will be discovered if people never think about the whys and what-ifs. Our curiosity led us to a path of discoveries within ourselves that gave us many opportunities that not everyone had. Opportunity is part of a formula that can lead you to success. Without the right formula, success is hard to achieve. We can have all the opportunities another person had, but we see how some people faced failures. Our rough beginnings with the guidance of our beloved parents helped us have a good reaction toward challenges.

We grew up facing a number of challenges, and at times we truly struggled. One thing we learned is everything will happen and be directed based on how you look at things. Our challenges in life have taught us to have a better perspective toward the struggles we faced. You can push yourself to be positive all the time, but if you don't have the right perspective, you might be walking on the wrong path. We both believe that success is a formula of curiosity, opportunity, perseverance, and perspective.

One way we can benefit from our curiosity is that it gave us a good sense of observation. Observation will lead you to open doors of many possibilities that can satisfy your curiosity. Life is full of science. Being in the travel market for more than a decade, I have noticed that many companies in almost all industries—not only in Bahrain but within the region—have preferred to copy rather than be creative or come up with different ideas. This became a trend. Whatever becomes viral, everyone begins doing. Social media was a great instrument to take this into full swing. Becoming an influencer" then became a big thing with sharing person-to-person experiences, and everyone started to copy others and follow what's trending to be "in"—just like a fashion trend.

When Spring started, the travel industry was already mature, and the competition was tremendous. Plunging in was not easy, but we managed. Things have somehow become predictable based on key players in the market, and trends are based on the impression of what the key players do most often. Since the beginning, we have aimed to maintain our goal to be unique and offer new movements.

Through years of exposure in the market, I have gained adequate experiences to observe well and be able to read and predict market trends. Since we started, taking our lead has always been one of our top priorities. The technology has drastically taken over and automated the businesses worldwide. Changes and trends are changing so fast that you are either left behind or you keep up and lead.

Our observations since we were first exposed to this industry have taught us to see the concerns that need to be addressed. Those concerns were the foundation of our strong marketing, which played a major role in where we are right now. It is indeed fascinating to see how marketing makes businesses lucrative. In the early stages of our start-up, we invested a lot in our marketing preparations and plans, as we were confident that it would be one of our express lifts to success from our start-up. Our marketing was carved up into two parts: an initiator and an innovator. With the mature market, imitating the rest would not put us in our desired stand, and we wouldn't be able to hit our targets to bring new ideas and take the lead.

As Tom Hayes has been quoted: "Without authenticity, we are only a poor imitation of someone else." The imitation is at its finest in any industry anywhere. People nowadays tend to either rework or plainly copy what's commonly available in the market, but it is still the same—just a copy or a different version. We envisioned Spring to be unique, so we joined the market not as a follower but as an initiator of a new idea. We mainly focus on bringing exceptional and unique marketing ideas.

To begin with, the tour arrangements in our country were traditional, and there was no specific branding among travel agencies. Over the years, Ahmed's organizing skills have notably improved, and this contributed eminently to our marketing, advertisements, and operations. Spring Travel was the first travel company in the country to have a specific branding. Every detail of our branding is well thought out and prepared beforehand. Prior to our official launching, we made sure that every specific detail was applied in all department materials: from office stationery, office interiors, staff uniforms, and advertising materials.

Our unified branding added great value to our professional business image. Our branding had given a good awareness of our presence to travelers and the rest of the market. After we launched, many noticed the unique design of our office interior, and most were left impressed with the details of artistry in preparations. Every customer and guest who visited our office gave us compliments about the interior design of our office, and remarkably, our branding remined in their impression of us. Our branding served as our manual guide and helped us keep track of everything we do. It also helped create our identity in the market, starting with the color itself.

We had chosen a specific color that was not used by any travel company in the market rather than using the common colors, which were mainly red, orange, and blue. Some people wondered why we put so much effort into our branding. One reason was to showcase ourselves.

People will view you how you present yourself. We don't get the chance to change the first impression we give to anyone, so we want to make sure first impressions of us are remembered well and leave a lasting impression. Because we were new to a mature market, we aimed to make a grand entrance, and so we did. Spring Travel will be always remembered by our brand color: apple green. Our branding is one of the things that we are truly proud of, as we have seen the impact it leaves on the people and the market itself.

Every advertising piece we make is designed according to our branding style. We keep concept formats unified. Not only is this pleasing to the eyes, but it retains the class and elegance of the design. With the vast use of the internet, we opt to widely promote our services through social media channels rather than sending bulk SMS texts to all telecom providers and sending leaflets via post. Our social media posts are all coordinated designs according to our branding. We try to make our ads as simple as possible with a touch of elegance, which has been known to be our branding trademark style.

Every season we select a design concept for our social media content. Our concept is always designed based on what a traveler would want to see and know in order to make the decision to book travel with us. Every photo we use is not just to show the main attraction but to give you reasons why you should visit. We are the first travel company to confidently publish the photos of our tour captains in every group advertisement. It is not only to adorn our advertisement posts but to show our transparency to our travelers. Additionally, knowing the person leading the group throughout their entire trip is a great relief and comfort to travelers.

> *When people start copying your style, you know that something must be happening.*
>
> — James Hetfield

The advancement of technology is one of our great tools to map out our marketing promotions, like boosting up our social media presence, but we have also made a huge investment in our marketing giveaways. Alongside our branding, we have selected special gifts that we can hand out to our customers. It is not just a giveaway but giving them a souvenir from us that they can use for keeps and will remind them of their trip experiences and memories traveling with us.

We usually distribute our giveaways during the trip so our travelers can use them. Giving out these gifts is not just marketing. Seeing everyone in the group using the gifts during the trip makes the group look pleasing and stand out in the crowd, giving us a visible identity. People can recognize a Spring Group from far away, and it also makes it easy for our tour captains to locate our travelers whether at the airport or other destinations.

In the Middle East , summer is the best and most awaited period of the year for everyone in the industry, as it is the busiest time of year—the time when everyone sells out. Given the importance of the season, we do not go with the usual advertising of our packages through distribution of common flyers. We opted to create a new way to do things and made our own promotional materials with our summer season packages tour guide to showcase our group packages.

Our packages tour guide is not only a compilation of offered packages. It also includes a compilation of necessary information. We believe that transparency is of great importance to gain the utmost trust of the travelers, making it easier to market our services. The more they see from you, the more they understand how you do things, and the more they trust your capabilities. Aside from our tour packages, our summer packages tour guide contains updated information about our destinations and interesting tips for your visit, which we research thoroughly and gather every year. This includes do and don'ts, weather, and currency information. The most important part of it is showing the trip information, which all of our travelers find it quite helpful.

Planning a trip can be a headache, as you need to check everything ahead of time, so we designed our packages tour guide to give peace of mind to our travelers. They get to know details of every trip, as we publish the itinerary information of every package. We designed it to be easy to use not only for travelers but for our team as well.

Before the trip, our travelers get to prepare well. After the trip, all of our travelers return home with smiles on their faces. Our summer packages tour guide has become one of our yearly tradition, as we are overwhelmed by how people respond to it. Many travelers visit our office just to get a copy of it. Some travelers take many copies and distribute them to family and friends, and some even display it in their respective businesses.

There have been numerous cases when people approach us and tell us, "Oh, I know you! I've seen you in the catalogue!" Others have said, "Your face is very familiar; I think I've seen you in a magazine or something."

There are also people who will just approach us and ask about bookings and packages. This happens not only to us but also our tour captains and other team members. They get to share the same spotlight we do.

Our summer packages tour guide is distributed to all customers around the Kingdoms of Bahrain and Saudi Arabia. It is amazing how the Spring packages tour guide is distributed all around the country, as our dear travelers have been of great help with distribution. It served its purpose in the market well, and all our hard work and the effort taken to prepare it are absolutely worth it.

The story of our tour captains is a long one to tell. They are one of our main assets, and we are proud of each one of them. Every tour captains also carries our branding. On every trip, they are provided with a distinct uniform that they wear for the entire trip, making it easy for our travelers to recognize them among the group. Their uniform is specifically designed to distinctively stand out in their group and other groups they might encounter during their trip.

Our tour captain is fully geared up with travel accessories he may need during the trip. We designed a sling bag for him to carry his important travel documents and sometimes a few surprises for the group members. Our tour captains are not fully geared up with our accessories, but they have sound knowledge of handling groups. Sustainability is one of our topmost priorities, and one of the main pipelines for our sustainability is the performance of our tour captains. We make sure that each one of them adheres to our policies and procedures to guarantee the excellent quality of our services.

Our tour captains are not just our captains. They are some of our best marketing representatives. They engage directly with our travelers. Our branding doesn't stop with how we gear up our tour captains with their uniforms and travel accessories. It extends to how they communicate and attend to every traveler in their groups. We have a protocol that each tour captain must strictly follow, not only to make sure he is not missing out on anything for the trip but, most importantly, to keep the tour coordinated between himself and the travelers.

We have prepared a series of message templates that tour captains can send to every traveler in order to introduce themselves, answer inquiries, share necessary information, and give relevant reminders. We have a series of processes that they must follow in order to make sure everything is in order.

It begins with introducing themselves to our travelers when they start to communicate at least a week before departure. All reminders and guidelines sent to travelers have been prepared ahead of time and personally checked by me and Ahmed. The messages sent to our travelers contain the necessary information about their trips, such as flight details, hotel information, and tour itinerary. Before the tour, every traveler is well informed by the tour captains, and at times they even help some travelers to prepare for their trips.

Most of them receive a variety of questions: What type of clothes should I bring? Where should I exchange my money? Should I do it here in Bahrain or when we arrive at the airport? How much money should I bring? What kind of food do they have there? Should I bring this kind of food? Is there any place there that I can buy this and that? Where is it cheaper to buy this and that? And there are so many other questions that it's not possible to include them all in this book.

The questions and inquiries we receive from travelers is one of the main reasons we invest in the betterment of our tour captains. They must be updated with the information of their handled destinations. Handling groups is not only answering their questions. It takes remarkable leadership skills to do it well. We want to make sure that all of our tour captains are competent to lead our groups.

Alongside our branding, it doesn't only go through the organization management but also with the knowledge requirements of every team member. We provide annual required trainings and seminars for our tour captains to keep them all knowledgeable and fully prepared for anything that may happen on their trips. All trainings and seminars are outsourced and conducted by experts. From the basic traveling guide to emergency safety handling, they are well trained, as the safety and comfort of our travelers is one of our top priorities.

Our tour captains, like the rest of our team members, possess the Spring attitude, making every booking and trip a fun and memorable one. We also started as travelers and then tour captains. It was a great advantage for us to be both, and it gave us a great point of view to form our Spring attitude.

I once read somewhere: "Your smile is your logo. Your personality is your business card. How you leave others feeling after an interaction becomes your trademark." I couldn't agree more, as this sentiment is absolutely correct. Therefore, we are very selective with our tour captains. Not everyone has the personality a tour captain should possess. We cannot please everyone, but it takes a great personality to handle different expectations and satisfy all of them.

With our regular trainings, our tour captains are trained to handle a variety of situations and trained on how to deal with and properly treat every traveler. Handling a group honestly takes a lot of effort and is tiring, but our tour captains always keep smiling. It is not only leadership skills and knowledge that makes someone a good tour captain; it is also their dedication. A passion for doing this job enables a person to be a great tour captain.

We are fortunate enough to have good-humored and professional tour captains, and this makes them different from other tour captains in the market. After every trip, I remind our tour captains that our goal is to create a great story and give meaning to everything they do. This way, their interactions and their trips with us become treasured memories for the travelers.

Not only that we take them places, but we give them lasting memories. As majority of our trips are groups of families, we do our best to make their travel experience with us one of the best in their lifetimes.

People are going to copy your product if you build great stuff. Just because Yahoo has a search box doesn't make it Google.

— Evan Spiegel

Destinations. Yes, it is always the best and most challenging part of what we do. As travelers ourselves, we are taking much of our time thinking about where to go. Our group destinations are designed not only to go to places but to make it worth every dinar that travelers will spend. Sometimes, when people can't decide, they just go and visit the same place that they have visited before. Going back to our marketing plan—yes, it is like our holy guide—if we promote the same destinations over and over, then it will be the same as following others. We don't want to fall into that; instead, we build our own blue ocean so we can have new areas to work. As we introduced ourselves, we called ourselves innovators. We create and initiate new areas where other people don't work. We do extensive market studies and introduce new destinations to the market. We mix destinations that would be worth not only the money but the time of traveling.

For example: in Europe you pay a lot of money for the flight just to visit one country. When we launched multiple European destinations, it spread like wildfire and became a hit. There was really a good response from the market for packages with a minimum of three or four different countries to be visited. Because the majority of our travelers are groups of families, we always put in our priorities and concerns that every member of the family must be able to enjoy the destinations and will be able to travel comfortably for the entire journey. Their entertainment and relaxation during the tour is important to us. If they are uncomfortable, it is not only a problem for our travelers but also for the tour captain who will have the task of settling the situation and at the same time making sure of everyone's comfort and addressing their concerns.

People travel to relax and enjoy the moment, not to be stressed and uncomfortable while going around because the trip is not well-suited for their physical capacity. We select destinations not only because of popularity but because of convenience and safety for every traveler. We also consider the activities that are available at the destinations we propose, as, again, we consider that every member of the family must be able to enjoy things. We strive to have a variety of options available to keep the group entertained. We don't want to leave them bored, sitting and just looking around.

Before we promote a new destination, we first visit it by ourselves, check the facilities, and try out the activities. We want to ensure that the trip is worth introducing to the market. We aim to bring our travelers to places they have never been before. We were able to introduce and promote new destinations to the market, and people were booking right then and there!

Through our social media accounts, we gave them a sneak preview of what to see through our own personal experiences, making us reliable service providers. We promoted places we had actually been and not just because we could offer the trips. Our personal experiences were the best advertisement. People could see actual videos and photographs of the destinations. People could see that we were familiar with these places because we'd been there. We were the most reliable storytellers of our own experiences, leaving people in awe. They would then ask the question: "When are you going to pay a visit?"

In 2017 we launched a campaign called "Yes, We Can!" using the hashtag #yes_we_can in our social media presence. We even launched a video with our team members and our tour captains saying it in different languages. The campaign was about promoting and celebrating our first summer season's success. There were some people, especially our competitors, who judged us and didn't think we would make it. They were sure we'd eventually pack our bags and go home, but we proved them wrong with our successful summer season.

It was quite a challenge with all the pressure, as we didn't expect the response would be so enormous. We were on a cloud nine. We made a grand entrance when we plunged into the market, and we did justice to the great first impressions we received.

What made us even happier was all the travelers who celebrated with us. Our travelers willingly joined us in our video footage, giving a thumbs-up and cheerfully exclaiming: "Yes, we can!" after being asked, "Can we?"

Oh, yes, we can! Some may say that it was just an expression, but among our travelers, it became a trademark for Spring. A slogan can mean a lot, and for us, it gave us a wide horizon that yes, we can do many great things, and we are limitless. Yes, we can do it. Yes, we can make it. Yes, we can take you places. You can name it, and it gives you the answers. It was a strong campaign that boosted both the company and us personally.

Our travelers have proven that it wasn't just a campaign. They enjoyed the kind of travel experience we had promised them. For years, many groups of families have been very loyal and traveled with us many times. We have even seen how their families grow.

Even today, we still use and promote the slogan. We received some videos and photos from our travelers using the slogan as a caption or happily exclaiming it aloud. It is heartwarming to watch—a simple phrase that marked their hearts and minds as a way to remember Spring.

In order to refresh the market following the #yes_we_can campaign, we decided to create an icon that represents us. As a result, we gave birth to a cheerful icon we named Mr. Springer. His introduction caused a big buzz in the market. We are proud to say that we are the first and only travel and tours service company to create such an icon. We have created a lot of promotional materials, such as Mr. Springer joining some of the departing and arriving trips. Mr. Springer sometimes joined the tour captains' incentive trips, and he is always present at our events to bring joy and create smiles.

The children loved Mr. Springer. Normally, little children are afraid of mascots, but with our Mr. Springer, kids would run toward him, and some even grabbed and hugged him while asking their parents to take their photos with him.

It wasn't only the children who adored him but also the young at heart. We have seen many people take photos with Mr. Springer. We were over the moon after the warm welcome Mr. Springer received. He not only created a buzz but bolstered our presence in the market. Our minds were blown by how our travelers appreciated and loved our icon, so we invested to promote him.

Mr. Springer soon became the new face of the Spring brand. We have added him in our all marketing and promotional materials. Mr. Springer then became the main content of our social media posts, and all promotional advertising materials are modeled by him still today. He has been to many places as well—anywhere we are promoting. He has even worn the traditional clothes of the destinations we have promoted, making people love him more and more. His cuteness spreads happiness not only to us but to all who see him. We have had guests and partners visit our office, and upon seeing him, Mr. Springer stole the spotlight.

He is truly contagious. He makes people smile, and some end up giggling and then laughing as they are so amazed by our icon. Some of our guests even acted like little children, grabbing and hugging him for a photo. To us, he isn't just an icon but a symbol of our commitment to bring happiness to people. He helped us deliver and made it real. It's no wonder Mr. Springer is everywhere now.

It is better to fail in originality that to succeed in imitation.

— Herman Melville

In early 2018, our #yes_we_can campaign and Mr. Springing were still making noise, so we launched our summer season packages tour guide with Mr. Springer on the cover. There are no words to explain the overwhelming demand we received from all travelers. Our phone lines rang nonstop, and we worked around the clock to attend all inquiries. The bookings for our summer groups that year sold out so quickly that we needed to launch additional groups.

With the massive demand from the travelers, the competition grew more intense in the market. We began seeing numerous travel companies taking the same path we had. They copied everything from our promotional advertisements to our packages and itineraries, and even their tour captains dressed like ours. With our own eyes, we witnessed them in the airport using the same routine as ours, handing departing and welcome gift to travelers.

Most of our loyal travelers have noted it and even shared it with us. Honestly, it didn't bother us. Instead, we were flattered, and we are happy to see that others followed in our footsteps because we have proven that our marketing plan and strategies were effective. That is what enabled us to take the lead and made others want to follow.

We can share, and it's no secret because people can see how we do things. I have always believed in one thing in life: Anyone can follow you. Anyone can try to do the things you do. But no one can do it the same exact way as you. Your passion and dedication can never be imitated by anyone else.

I look at it as being similar to cooking. Even if you publish your recipe and teach someone to cook the dish step-by-step, it will never taste the same as how you cook it by yourself.

Anyone can imitate, but that was never on our minds. Since our younger years, we always preferred to work hard to build our own blue ocean that would let us have all the possibilities and no norms that would control us. Instead, we directed it and defined it. We built Spring as a creative company, bringing in our own interesting and fresh ideas. Creativity means not copying. After all, we are gratified to see with our own eyes that all of our efforts, those sleepless nights, those times we were far away from our families, and all our sacrifices have been worthwhile. Everything paid off, and we are truly doing things the right way. Today, we continue to work hard to keep bringing new ideas and creativity to all travelers.

And yes, we don't follow. We lead!

Chapter 5

Where Are We Today?

Success is a journey, not a destination.

— Arthur Ashe

Nothing happens overnight. Bahrain is a small island country, and the main source of income is fishing and farming. We might have not done fishing and farming as our jobs, but we have been influenced by the inspiration you could get from the people doing it.

Reaching our goals wasn't easy and took pure hard work. We have been left with life lessons of perseverance and patience. Success is a never-ending process, and it is a journey of achieving our goals one by one. It takes time as well, as there is no instant success. There might have been some people who have been lucky enough to be successful at a young age, but it's still a series of processes and preparations.

As we have mentioned, change is the only permanent thing in life. We can be successful in reaching a goal today, but who knows what may come tomorrow. We see success as a series of achievements. Reaching your goal is one success, and that may be followed by another and another. Looking back to our beginning at the first meeting we had, we can say that everything that we brainstormed and discussed for such a long time has happened exactly as we wanted it to. In fact, it was even better than what we expected.

We are just two simple men raised in a humble family who grew up with curiosity about how life can be surprising if we explore beyond to see what life can give us. It hasn't been an easy life for our parents, so we want them to have that moment and see their children achieving their dreams and goals.

We cannot thank our parents enough for their tender love and care. In our hearts, we push ourselves to be better people as a way to reciprocate everything our parents did for us. Our every success isn't only ours; it is theirs as well. Our humble beginnings gave us the strong urge to dream of something more, something out of the box. We pushed ourselves to do something our parents would be so proud of.

Yes, we dedicate everything we do mostly for our parents and family. We will never be where we are today if our beloved parents did not raise us well and teach us such compassion. Our late father has been our inspiration. No matter how hard life was, he never let it put him down. He was indeed the paragon of strength and showed us that nothing is impossible if you want to do something. Our dear mother has taught us to treat every person with a warm heart, just as we would our own sibling, and to never look down on anyone.

Through the storms in our lives, our beloved parents have taught us well and molded us to be genuinely good people with the utmost compassion, dedication, and optimism. Both our parents gave us treasures that can never be equal to any amount of money.

Our rough beginning ironed us to seek better opportunities that would improve our lives. However, our desire was not simply to improve our lives but to honor the hardship of our beloved parents and be able to give them the life they deserved. When you have that devotion, it leads you to have a strong will to strive more to do better, and many opportunities will come in your way.

From our experiences, we learned that when you just go with the flow, you may never see the success you want because you did not exert any effort or try to look for ways to improve yourself. Everything begins within yourself. Without the right behaviors, it seems impossible to achieve your goals.

As we have said before, success is a series of formulas and a never-ending process. You walk on a path in your life not to go to a destination but toward a path on your journey to success. One of the behaviors we have learned in order to stand out is to be the early bird. By being the first and being early, we believe you get to enjoy more blessings and have a higher chance of seizing the day than anyone else. This desire grew within us, and it is a behavior we keep doing and aiming for in our lives. Now that we have our business, we still apply the same behavior. Most days, my brother is in our office at seven o'clock in the morning, as he gets the chance to do many things with his fresh mind when more ideas are coming.

This behavior is one of the main roots of how we do things, and it became a discipline that we teach to our children and all team members. It is a simple behavior that develops a good self-discipline. If you continue practicing it, it allows you to enjoy many things in life. Because it has been proven, we applied it in our structure as a must behavior and discipline for every team member of Spring to have.

As we were planning our structure for Spring, one of the things that we considered was that all members must possess the same enthusiasm as us. They must be all ready to join the battle in the field, as we are introducing our company in a very mature industry with many alternatives, some of which had already built a strong foundation.

We were a newbie in the market, so how would people trust us? How would we make ourselves known? Spring was a product of our curiosity and our strong drive of passion and devotion to do something new. Before launching Spring, we had strategically planned our grand entrance, as we were aware of the competition. We had been known in the market, and somehow travelers had known us and our credibility in the business. We were able to build a better connection to people whom we'd traveled with. In addition, Mohamed's longer exposure in the market gained him more support, not only with the travelers but from tour service suppliers, hotels, and airlines.

Being the first or the early bird is not enough. It must be combined with a strong personality. Interacting with different people and our exposure in the market greatly leveled up our confidence; thus, it made our personalities interesting in combination with our personal background during our younger years.

Personality is not something that can be bought in the shop. It takes years of experiences to build. I would say that we are both lucky to have had many opportunities to gain confidence, yet we have always kept our feet on the ground. Our personalities are one of the main leverages to our success. They have helped us build good relationships with many people, especially in the industry. They have opened doors to have strong support from our suppliers, and it's not only because our business has been doing well.

Mohamed has more exposure than I do within the industry, and with his appealing personality, he managed to build good relationships with many people from different travel companies, airlines, and tour operators, giving him a good bridge of networks. His personality was the linking bridge to the start of good business relationships. But what made people trust him was that he has shown that he is a good partner in the industry. Mohamed's thinking is admirable, as when he starts doing business, he shows that he knows what he is doing with all the nitty-gritty of the business. Mohamed's credibility in the market has gained him the personal trust of key people from the airlines, destination management companies, and other travel companies.

When we launched Spring, we received positive support from all travel service suppliers and airlines. We were honored when they attended our official opening in 2015. Major airlines have known Mohamed's level of professionalism and reliability, and as a result, they have taken Spring Travel to be the most professional travel company. This means we are able to keep up and follow up all group time limits and issue tickets on time. The good connections he built with suppliers gave us the advantage of offering good rates for great packages to travelers. Our suppliers have seen the good progress of our sales, which has enabled us to be one of their valued partners and give strong support to their businesses.

In 2016 Spring Travel was the only non-IATA (International Air Transport Association) travel company that was selected and invited by Qatar Airways to join their familiarization trip to the Maldives. This was followed by many more invitations. In 2019 we were recognized and honored by Emirates and were given a certificate of appreciation for being one of their outstanding non-IATA travel agents.

Mohamed has shared our success not only with us but with our hardworking staff who give their best efforts and work despite of the heavy workload and pressure they face. Our success is their success as well. None of it would happen without their support. The strength of our team comes from every member of our team, and every member of our team runs for the same goal: our team's success.

Mohamed and I are thankful for every member of our team, as they give their hard work, and even their families support to us. There are times of difficulties, but they stay focused to keep our groups organized and help give satisfaction to our travelers.

In a short span of time, we garnered our success, and it wouldn't be possible without the compelling efforts and dedication of our team members, especially our tour captains who make our trips truly memorable for our travelers. We all work and support each other, hand in hand from the beginning to today. It could be great luck, but we consider it to be the greatest blessing from God that we managed to pull through with all the ups and downs of this adventurous journey.

In fact, our Spring family has grown bigger. We began this journey with a minimum of fifteen tour captains, and now we count more than sixty dedicated tour captains among our team. Since the beginning, we have received a lot of applications seeking to join our team. Our tour captains are geographically distributed within Bahrain but from different villages and cities, from different communities, and from different families and friends. This gives us good exposure within the entire country. Given that, many people have seen how we recognize the excellent performance of our tour captains. They are one of the keys to our success.

We consider our tour captains to be the final touch for every tour, as they will be accompanying and interacting with our travelers the entire tour. They are the ones who deliver the services we promote, and they share in the one-of-a-kind experiences we advertise to our customers. They create unforgettable travel memories to our every traveler.

Each tour captain takes care of his group. He attends to every concern, making sure everyone is comfortable and enjoying his or her trip. With the big responsibilities they carry every trip, we reward them by giving them an annual incentive trip for them to relax and enjoy traveling with their fellow tour captains. This makes us the first and only travel company to provide such an incentive to their team.

We had friends who were concerned about the benefits we were giving our tour captains, publishing their photos, promoting them, and making them popular. We do not believe in that, however, because we believe that we both have an equal opportunity. It's an opportunity for them and an opportunity for us. They have shown their support and served as some of our best marketing representatives. We obviously cannot force anyone to stay or leave, but we value and believe in the good relationships we have built.

We always have the best wishes for their endeavors, and we thank them for their efforts and time they've put in since joining us in our journey. They will be always part of our team. We dreamt of a better community, and we are glad that it happened through our tour captains.

We usually gather them for some sports activities, dinner, and events. Through the gatherings, a good camaraderie has been built. They started as colleagues, became friends, and have now become family. Our tour captains believe that they belong to us. It is fulfilling for us to see their relationships growing. Because of this, they actually built a club and named it Springers Club. It is truly an amazing feeling to be a part of connecting people and building a good community.

Train people well enough so they can leave, treat

them well enough so they don't want to.

— Richard Branson

Springers, our tour captains, have been some of our best marketing representatives. Additionally, to show our strong support for them, they have always been highlighted in our every campaign and their photos have always been at the forefront, promoting their popularity. We provide them efficient and orderly trainings and workshops aside from frequent gatherings, which are part of the major things in our business plan to encourage them and motivates them.

Spring Travel has become our best platform to enable us to contribute improvements to the community and to the industry. Remembering when we began, we were a small company who dreamt big—a small company with big visions of bringing change and creative ideas to the market. Spring is the product of our humble beginnings and experiences that cultivated us. Some may have doubted us, but we have proven our stand and credibility in the market. We built this company to be able to share our experiences and improve the quality of services in the market.

Our beginning was truly challenging, starting when we introduced our company. There was a question in our minds when we decided to open Spring: "What will make people change from a big, confident travel agency and come to Spring?" It was this challenging question that started everything.

We did not just show off and talk. We made a huge investment of effort, knowledge, time, and money. Our marketing was one of our strongest leverages for our rapid success. We believe in a marketing formula that if one customer is happy, that person will talk to twenty persons, and then those twenty persons will remember our name. They will either try our services or share the recommendation they heard. It becomes a domino effect, which is one reason for us to care so much to maintain high standards and provide excellent services to every customer.

When we began, we used a lot of promotions, such as putting our advertisement on road stands, creating our summer packages tour guide, and holding big events. We also believed that the new way of marketing was connecting you to me. We have since introduced different creative ideas to the market, like our icon, Mr. Springer, which has become the face of our branding.

We were also the first travel company to invest in travel accessories that we distribute during tours, and each giveaway is made to be useful during and after travel. Many of our travelers keep these items as souvenirs. We prefer to make that investment with giveaways rather than to spend money on a luxurious lifestyle showing off.

We prefer to focus on our work while we keep our feet firmly on the ground. This way, when the wind blows in, we are strong enough to withstand it. We are financially strong and capable. Being in this industry, one thing we have learned is if you want to stay longer and stronger, you need to make an investment. You don't think of big profit today; a small profit that covers the expenses will do. You need to keep the balance and not just look at the profit you will earn. Once you struggle, the next day you are out of the market. With little profit, you earn the trust and loyalty of your customers. They make you strong and help you stay in the business.

What makes us continue in this bad economic situation is that we are strong from the continuous support and patronage of our loyal customers who frequently traveled with us. There have been times when customers have found cheaper packages from other companies, but because of their internal connection with us, they chose to return to Spring and book their trip. They know the quality of our services, and they know that they will be well taken care of. That connection that they felt is the great result of our investments and efforts. Our investments turn into long-term relationships with our valued customers, and those relationships keep us stronger in the business.

Aside from the creative ideas we introduced to the market, we had an additional firsts—introducing new destinations: Antarctica and Argentina. Mohamed, together with Omar Farooq, a well-known videographer and social media influencer, embarked on their adventurous trip to Antarctica, making us the first travel company to visit and promote the end of the world, the Earth's southernmost continent. It was exciting to see how people followed the series of teasers and guessed where the location would be.

When we invited Omar to join us on this trip of a lifetime, he had no clue where it would be. Knowing the reputation of Spring, he did not hesitate to join without knowing the destination, but Mohamed gave him some hints that it would be freezing. A few days after he met Mohamed, we sent Omar a block of ice with a rolled paper inside. He covered it in his Instagram stories while he waited for the ice block to melt to discover where Spring would be taking him. Omar revealed our epic adventure through his Instagram stories, and many were surprised.

Looking back through records, we discovered there had only been one Bahraini to visit the continent as part of the Environmental Citizenship Program of Bahrain Women Association. Her name was Amal Al Saffar, and she also showed support for our expedition. It was indeed exciting and historic for us, as we would be the first travel company to discover what Antarctica has to offer for tourism in our current market.

The adventure created a buzz and was even featured in newspapers. The coverage on our social media accounts gained a lot of attention, and sparked interest in a lot of people. The goal of our trip was to bring awareness to the alarming effects of global warming and climate change. We have to protect our environment. It is not only humans who will be affected, but all wonderful living animals around the world suffer too.

If you have a dream, don't just sit there. Gather
courage to believe that you can succeed and leave no
stone unturned to make it a reality.

— Dr. Roopleen Prasad

Within our first two years of operations, Spring Travel became one of the leading outbound travel companies in the market. In 2017 we had served and assisted more than ten thousand travelers for their trips. We had more than three thousand who joined our summer tour groups. In 2018 we had almost five thousand travelers who joined a total of 129 summer groups, and we introduced new destinations to Europe (Croatia and Slovenia) and Asia (South Korea, Japan, Nepal, Philippines, and India). Because of the growing demand for European destinations, we had earned credibility for visa assistance with a high percentage of approval, which raised the number of travelers who joined our Europe summer groups. We became one of the specialists in the market. There were actually too many people calling and visiting us for consultations as they searched for recommendations.

In 2019 we had arranged and exhibited a total of 144 successful groups during the summer season. We also introduced new destinations to Portugal, Russia, Lithuania, Latvia, Estonia, Albania, Montenegro, Macedonia, Serbia, and China. Aside from groups of families and individuals, we catered and teamed up with various corporations from different sectors such as Grnata Real Estate, Ammar Optician, IKEA Bahrain, Al Wisam School,

Dadabhai Holidays, Spire Travel, Delta Holidays, Dadabhai Travel, Al Abraaj Restaurant, *Akhbar Al Khaleej* newspaper, and more.

Additionally, Spring is the first travel company to invest in and conduct opening and closing ceremony events for the summer season. During our opening ceremony, we launch our summer tour packages and begin distributing of our summer guide. During the closing ceremony, which we usually hold at the Al Ayam Media Center Conference Hall, we celebrate the success of all our groups and distribute awards to our suppliers and to our team members who supported us wholeheartedly during the hectic summer operations.

2020 marked the beginning of our sixth year, and we launched our summer groups earlier than the usual. On January 20, 2020, we launched our 2020 summer groups and hosted the official opening of our new office, which was attended by representatives from different airlines and our partners. We were also honored by the presence of Senan Ali Jaberi, the official representative from Bahrain Tourism and Exhibitions Authority Office.

No matter how small you start, always dream and think big. If you start with small thoughts then you will stay with small thoughts.

— Stephen Richards

With all the initiatives and creativity that Spring Travel has brought and keeps bringing in the market, Spring has become one of the benchmarks and one of the strongest contenders in the market. It is our pleasure and honor to bring improvements to our travel industry. Our first five years have been a remarkably a great success for us and for every member of our team. Our first five years of operations have marked our great standing and stability in the market.

Briefly, the Spring way to keep our company on top of the market is by offering unique services, having competitive prices, and using indirect marketing, as well as our amazing tour captains and human resources team. It's about our well-built branding. Also, we don't worry. Instead, we are truly flattered by competitors who follow our lead. We might worry when they stop.

To dream is to have a chest filled with stars, a mind
captivated by possibilities and a heart enveloped in
imagination.

— Anastasia Bolinder

Today, Spring Travel is unbeatable and unstoppable as we continue to foster new initiatives and bring interesting creativity to the market with a global network of more than sixty tour captains and nearly twenty office staff team members who reach all continents. No matter our position, we still work round the clock, and we don't stop working on improvements. It is not only about doing it as our work, but it has been our passion to challenge ourselves to bring something new. Time flies, and changes are inevitable. Our success inspires us to keep going on this journey and to achieve more and more, as we strived to reach our goals.

Our rapid success was truly life changing. We look at it as a great blessing from God. Our journey has just started, and we will never stop dreaming. We plan our actions and keep focused for today, for tomorrow, and for the future. Our journey will be a model for us to keep going and for our children to live by as an inspiration and motivation. We want to share our journey with everyone so that it may serve as an inspiration for others to seize opportunity and start their own journeys to success.

There are five important things for living a successful and fulfilling life: never stop dreaming, never stop believing, never give up, never stop trying, and never stop learning.

— Roy Bennett

We have many dreams to plan and achieve. Now is just the beginning. We still have many targets and goals to reach. We take our start as motivation to keep going and spare no effort in improving ourselves to be able to contribute more and change for the betterment of ourselves and Spring.

You may wonder why we always start with ourselves. We strongly believe that everything follows the circle of influence. It starts from us and our control and goes out to our circle of concern. We, ourselves, are the foundation of what we have for our present and what the future holds. Spring is a product of what we wanted—a company that allows us to make our dreams come true.

Spring gave us the opportunity to cross paths with people we never knew would be part of us, part of our growing family, and part of our dream community. Spring is our incredible journey that led us to a path where we met wonderful people who helped us build our dreams. There might be some roadblocks along our way, but we have a great team who walks with us hand in hand and rallies around us to reach our dreams and plans.

Life has given us way more than our expectations, and there are still a lot of surprises and opportunities to explore. Let's go, and we'll take you to places.

Spring Creative Management Team

Mohamed Al Hamad, Chief Executive Officer

Ahmed Al Hamad, Deputy Chief Executive Officer

Hasan Sabba, Sales and Marketing Manager

Husain Rastam, Business Development Manager

Spring Creative Team

Zainab Al Durazi, Reservation Supervisor

Fatema Al Mudaweb, Reservations Officer

Mohamed Ameen, Reservations Officer

Maitham Husain, Reservations Officer

Ruqaya Sayed Mahdi, Operations Officer

Charisse Ann Lim, Assistant Business Development Manager

Shahul Hameed, Accounts Manager

Man Bahadur, Logistics Services

Muslem Al Taiban, Al-Ahsa, Kingdom of Saudi Arabia, Branch Supervisor

Husain Al Qattan, Al-Ahsa, Kingdom of Saudi Arabia, Branch Reservations Officer

Mohammed Al Qattan, Al-Ahsa, Kingdom of Saudi Arabia, Branch Reservations Officer

Fatema Al Sulaiman, Qatif, Kingdom of Saudi Arabia, Branch Reservations Officer

Ruqaya Al Muhaishi, Qatif, Kingdom of Saudi Arabia, Branch Reservations Officer

About the Authors

Mohamed Al Hamad is the chief executive officer of Spring Travel, and Ahmed Al Hamad is the co-founder and deputy chief executive officer. They are passionate travelers turned innovative entrepreneurs. They are the phenomenal dynamic duo behind Spring Travel's success. With their impeccable partnership, they work hard not to follow but to lead with their creativity and aim to bring happiness to every traveler.

Afterword

"It takes two to tango." This is the best description I could think of when I collaborated with the Al Hamad brothers for this book. When they first approached me for this project, I didn't hesitate to accept, as I knew that it would be an interesting project. I have read many success stories, but what makes theirs interesting is that they are two different people of different personalities who managed to pull through all challenges in their lives together and built Spring Travel.

It was quite challenging. I knew that I would struggle at some point, and I almost gave up because of the little time we could all spare. As we went deep into their beginnings and shared ideas about how things with the book would go, I confirmed that my first impression was right.

Most of the time, I was just listening while they shared their story. That's when I realized how brilliant their minds are, and it's truly fascinating how well they complement each other. Their beloved parents and family must have been so proud of them, as we all are. Ideas just come out naturally from them, and if the right person listens, which is mostly the Spring Team, then with the efforts of everyone, that idea comes to life.

Their story moved me. It gave me the motivation and encouragement to challenge myself, and I believe that it will do the same for anyone who reads this book. The Al Hamad brothers have shown us that success is no accident at all. It takes a lot of effort and dedication plus the support of your loved ones to achieve it. They both are the epitome of perseverance. It is impossible not to succeed if you work hard and give your massive dedication to it no matter what comes along your way. Admittedly, they had down times and needed to make some sacrifices, but the results are enviably worth every bit of it.

Their story has shown that they didn't just wish themselves to where they are standing right now. They dreamed, planned, and worked hard for everything they have. Now they left us the dare questions: Will you let yourself just sit and wait? Will you just babysit excuses and cry for success later?

It is indeed a privilege to collaborate with them, and it was truly an honor to be part of this book. They both gave me a fair challenge, and they have guided me and shown me that it is possible, and I will succeed too. I am highly confident that you will be inspired as well by their success and the lessons they learned from their challenges. It wasn't just a story being told. They left us with the certainty of: "Yes! We Can!"

Charisse Ann Lim

Assistant Business Development Manager

Glossary

Alhamdulilah. An Arabic phrase translated as, "Thank God."

Eid al-Adha. A Muslim festival marking the culmination of the annual pilgrimage to Mecca.

Hajj. An annual Islamic pilgrimage to Mecca, Saudi Arabia, the holiest city for Muslims. It is a mandatory religious duty for Muslims that must be carried out at least once in their lifetime by all adult Muslims who are physically and financially capable of undertaking the journey and can support their family during their absence. (https://en.wikipedia.org/wiki/Hajj)

hamla. A campaign for Islamic pilgrimage. Also known as a group of people assembled visiting holy places.

Husaini. An Arabic poetry expressing the incident of Karbala in the year 680.

IATA. International Air Transport Association

KSA. Kingdom of Saudi Arabia

Ma'atam. A dedicated venue for conducting mourning for Imam Husain (the grandson of the Prophet Mohamed).

Manama. The capital of the Kingdom of Bahrain.

Springer. An icon that represents Spring Travel and Tourism.

tour captains. Group leaders who manage Spring's groups of travelers.

Umrah. An Islamic pilgrimage to Mecca (the holiest city for Muslims, located in the Hejazi region of Saudi Arabia) that can be undertaken at any time of the year, in contrast to the Ḥajj, which has specific dates

according   to   the   Islamic   lunar   calendar.
(https://en.wikipedia.org/wiki/Umrah)

References

Chinese yin and yang. In Ancient Chinese philosophy, yin and yang is a concept of dualism, describing how seemingly opposite or contrary forces may actually be complementary, interconnected, and interdependent in the natural world, and how they may give rise to each other as they interrelate to one another. https://en.wikipedia.org/wiki/Yin_and_yang

Marcus Buckingham. He is a British author, motivational speaker and business consultant. https://en.wikipedia.org/wiki/Marcus_Buckingham

The 7 Habits of Highly Effective People. First published in 1989, is a business and self-help book written by Stephen Covey. Covey presents an approach to being effective in attaining goals by aligning oneself to what he calls "true north" principles based on a character ethic that he presents as universal and timeless. https://en.wikipedia.org/wiki/The_7_Habits_of_Highly_Effective_Peopl e

Plato. (May 21, 429 BC) Plato was an Athenian philosopher during the Classical period in Ancient Greece, founder of the Platonist school of thought, and the Academy, the first institution of higher learning in the Western world. https://en.wikipedia.org/wiki/Plato

Tree of Life. The Tree of Life in Bahrain is 9.75 meters high Prosopis cineraria tree that is over 400 years old. It is on a hill in a barren area of the Arabian Desert, 2 kilometers from Jebel Dukhan, the highest point in Bahrain, and 40 kilometers from Manama, the nearest city. The tree is abundantly covered in green leaves. https://en.wikipedia.org/wiki/Tree_of_Life_(Bahrain)

Leo Tolstoy. Count Lev Nikolayevich Tolstoy, usually referred to in English as Leo Tolstoy, was a Russian writer who is regarded as one of the greatest authors of all time. https://en.wikipedia.org/wiki/Leo_Tolstoy

John Heywood. Heywood was an English dramatist employed at the courts of Henry VIII and his daughter Mary I, but when Elizabeth I came to the throne in 1564, Heywood (a Roman Catholic) was forced to flee to Belgium, where he stayed for the rest of his life. He was important in the development of English comedy, specifically short comic dialogues known as interludes, but is now best remembered for his book of proverbs. https://www.bookbrowse.com/

Chris Paine. He is an American filmmaker and environmental activist. https://en.wikipedia.org/wiki/Chris_Paine

Roy T. Bennett. He is a thought leader and a positive thinker who loves sharing positive thoughts and creative insights. He inspires people to live up to their own potential of personal growth. Author of *The Light in the Heart.* https://www.beaninspirer.com/staying-within-comfort-zone-bad/

Archibald Marwizi. Archibald Marwizi is an author, trainer, life coach and speaker and was born in Gweru, Zimbabwe. https://www.goodreads.com/author/show/14084392.Archibald_Marwiz i

Walt Disney. He was an American entrepreneur, animator, voice actor and film producer. A pioneer of the American animation industry, he introduced several developments in the production of cartoons. https://en.wikipedia.org/wiki/Walt_Disney

Paul Wellstone. He was an American academic, author, and politician who represented Minnesota in the United States Senate from 1991 until he was killed in a plane crash in Eveleth, Minnesota, in 2002. https://en.wikipedia.org/wiki/Paul_Wellstone

Reba McEntire. Reba McEntire is an American country singer, songwriter, actress, and record producer.
https://www.brainyquote.com/quotes/reba_mcentire_457621

Hillary Clinton. She is an American politician, diplomat, lawyer, writer, and public speaker. She served as First Lady of the United States from 1993 to 2001, as a United States senator from New York from 2001 to 2009, and as the 67th United States secretary of state from 2009 until 2013. https://allauthor.com/quotes/54245/

Andrew Carnegie. He was a Scottish-American industrialist, and philanthropist. Carnegie led the expansion of the American steel industry in the late 19th century and became one of the richest Americans in history. https://www.cyclopt.com/blog/3+1-reasons-to-ensure-Teamwork-on-board

Fred DeVito. He is a nationally acclaimed star teacher. He holds a Bachelor's of Science in Physical Education and Health as well as an ACE Personal Trainer Certification, and brings 32 years of teaching experience to every class that he leads - first, through 22 years at the original Lotte Berk studio in New York, and then over nearly a decade at exhale and Core Fusion ® Barre. https://www.amazon.com/Fred-DeVito/e/B00Z3M862Y%3Fref=dbs_a_mng_rwt_scns_share

Emanuel James Rohn. He was professionally known as Jim Rohn, was an American entrepreneur, author and motivational speaker. https://www.jimrohn.com/your-productivity/

Albert Einstein. He was a German-born theoretical physicist who developed the theory of relativity, one of the two pillars of modern physics (alongside quantum mechanics). His work is also known for its influence on the philosophy of science. https://www.brainyquote.com/quotes/albert_einstein_106912

Sir Kenneth Robinson. He is a British author, speaker and international advisor on education in the arts to government, non-profits, education and arts bodies. https://www.goodreads.com/author/quotes/43940.Ken_Robinson

Tom Hayes. He is an American marketing executive, and is the founder of Joint Venture: Silicon Valley, a public-private economic consultancy and think tank. https://www.goodreads.com/author/quotes/31596.Tom_Hayes

James Howard Hatfield. He was an American author. He was the author of Fortunate Son, a book published in 1999 during the George W. Bush presidential campaign, 2000 that made serious allegations about George W. Bush. https://www.inspiringquotes.us/author/8192-james-hetfield

Evan Spiegel. Evan Thomas Spiegel is a French-American businessman who is the co-founder and CEO of the American social media company Snap Inc., which he created with Bobby Murphy and Reggie Brown while they were students at Stanford University. Spiegel was named the youngest billionaire in the world in 2015. https://en.wikipedia.org/wiki/Evan_Spiegel

Herman Melville. He was an American novelist, short story writer and poet of the American Renaissance period. Among his best-known works are his magnum opus, Moby-Dick (1851), and Typee (1846), a romantic account of his experiences of Polynesian life. https://www.brainyquote.com/quotes/herman_melville_121186

Arthur Ashe. He was an American professional tennis player who won three Grand Slam titles. https://www.goodreads.com/quotes/101537-success-is-a-journey-not-a-destination-the-doing-is

Richard Branson. He is a British business magnate, investor, author and philanthropist. He founded the Virgin Group in the 1970s, which controls more than 400 companies in various fields. https://www.virgin.com/richard-branson/look-after-your-staff

Dr Roopleen. She is a Motivational Counselor, Speaker, blogger, life enthusiast, author of 4 books and has contributed to many anthologies. https://www.goodreads.com/quotes/716480-if-you-have-a-dream-don-t-just-sit-there-gather

Stephen Richards. He is an author writing in the self-help genre. The first book he wrote in 1998 was in the true crime genre for Mirage Publishing. He has co-written a number of books with others, but now concentrates on writing in the mind, body, spirit subjects of Cosmic Ordering and mind power. http://www.wiseoldsayings.com/authors/stephen-richards-quotes/

Anastasia Bolinder. She is the author of the award-winning YA fantasy novel "From the Dust and "The Wolf and The Crimson Maiden!". https://www.goodreads.com/author/quotes/15903201.Anastasia_Bolinder